LAUGH LIKE A
JAMAICAN

LAUGH LIKE A
JAMAICAN

LENWORTH HENRY

iUniverse LLC
Bloomington

Laugh Like A Jamaican

iUniverse books may be ordered through booksellers or by contacting:

iUniverse LLC
1663 Liberty Drive
Bloomington, IN 47403
www.iuniverse.com
1-800-Authors (1-800-288-4677)

ISBN: 978-1-4917-0248-2 (sc)
ISBN: 978-1-4917-0249-9 (e)

Printed in the United States of America

iUniverse rev. date: 11/05/2013

CONTENTS

YES FATHER

As a young kid growing up, I was a guest at many denominational gatherings, and I was always intrigued by the uniqueness of each congregation's order of doing things. But as a Baptist, both the Anglican and the Catholic churches held the most mystery to me. The simple reason was that I loved to hear the chants, which I never was able to recite, let alone understand. Finally, I found a friend who was a master interpreter of all things Catholic and he led me through the process. In no time I could chant from here to eternity, but out of respect to the holy order and the protection of the innocence of my life educated friend, I will just give you an example of one of my favorites.

During communion, the father would go into this long monotone and the congregants would give the appropriate responses. I think it was done in Latin, as every strange word was thought to be. Father would hold the full cup of wine in his right hand and the plate of bread in the left. He would then proceed to raise both hands towards the, by now, drooling lips of his famished congregants, and he would recite the following, "Thou shall see it, smell it, and shall not taste of it." and the angry, impatient, but subdued response would be "Yes Father, wee know." Father would then do a pirouette and disappear; the wine and bread with him. And the faithful kept going back, Sunday after Sunday.

ME SHEG

The sermon for that Sunday was from the book of Daniel, that told the story of Nebuchadnezzar, the king of Babylon, who threw Shadrock, Meshak and Abendigo into the fiery furnace after they refused to bow down to the statue he built. It ended with all three miraculously escaping unharmed, due to divine intervention. The sermon must have held everyone spellbound, but it seemed sister Mildred was struck the hardest. The frequent repetition of the trio's rather exotic names seemed to have confused sister Mildred, who could well have been in her typical stupor and woke up only to hear what she thought she had heard. She left the service a sad and confused sister.

When she got home everyone noticed that the usually vivacious post worship disposition of Sister Millie was absent. When she was questioned, the heartbroken sister declared that the sermon was the cause of her discomfort, as in it, the parson delved into profanity and had repeatedly uttered some insulting words to the whole congregation, and he was actually quoting from the bible. When she was asked to say what it was, she reluctantly declared that the parson said and I quote, "Me sheg, you sheg, under bed we go." (Sheg is a minor curse word in Jamaica)

THE VERY PUSS

For those who do not know, puss is the pet reference to a domestic cat in Jamaica. Hardly anyone would use any other word when referring to a cat. What is incredible though, is how the same word used with strong emphasis, is the only sure way of chasing a cat away from just about any place, thing or activity. The following anecdote attests to that fact.

The parishioners at this particular church were often puzzled as to how their beloved parson was able, Sunday after Sunday, to maintain such high energy throughout the entire service and never appeared to be hungry and drained as they all usually were. They had always noticed that he would take the occasional break from the pulpit, especially during the singing of the hymns, but never read much into that. It so happened that the pastor had a secret that only deacon knew about; he always carried a plate of food to church every Sunday, and that explained his times out. But one fateful Sunday, parson had taken a few mouthfuls and left his plate in a corner in the vestibule when, lo and behold, the aroma of the tasty morsel reached a stray cat, who decided that this Sunday, he was not going to be satisfied with only the leftovers, he wanted the full entrée. In the middle of his sermon, which had nothing to do with giving praise or thanks, parson observed that this cat had gained entry through an open door and was about to raid his plate. His quick wit came immediately into play and the irrelevant subject of praise, cut into his original theme.

"Brothers and sisters." he suddenly exclaimed, "Everyone needs at times to praise the lord; The birds of the air, the fish of the seas." and seeing the cat removing the cover from his plate, he wasted no time to shout; "Even the very puss!" with the word puss, shouted out so loudly, that the poor cat made a dash for his life into the bushes. By now the congregation was so charged with praising the lord that they did not hear the dish cover fall to the ground. So parson was spared the embarrassment, and from that Sunday he made sure to secure that back door before he entered the pulpit, as he was not going to allow that stray to force him to give up his unholy semi-secret pastime.

WE SHALL GATHER BY THE RIVER

Pastor was livid on this particular Sunday as he was receiving more and more reports of his parishioners' propensity for the bottle. His sermon was entitled, 'Wine is a Mocker, and Strong Drink is Raging.' Guilt seemed to have kept the parishioners fairly restrained that morning, and parson was convinced that his point had reached home. So in conclusion, he declared that if he had the power, he would have taken all the alcohol in the world and he would have dumped it in the river.

As was his custom, whenever he thought that he had preached a convincing sermon, parson would specially ask deacon to lead the congregation in song. For the first time that Sunday, the entire congregation erupted as deacon raised the hymn 'We Shall Gather at the River.'

PRAISE THE LORD

Deacon had a jackass that he rode around every day. This donkey was trained to respond to religious commands only, so not many people would dare to try to borrow him, as they would other neighbors' It so happened, that one day parson was on a very important mission into the deep country and he was told that even if he drove his car, there were some parts of the road that were only accessible by foot. So he, for the first time, decided to engage the services of deacon's holy ass for the challenging trip. Before he was given the donkey, parson was briefed on the commands. He was told that whenever he wanted the ass to move, all he had to say was, 'praise the lord.' Whenever he needed him to stop, just say 'amen'. Parson thought that to be a no-brainer, him being a man of the cloth. So he thanked deacon and went on his righteous way, even testing the responses as he went by.

Parson was doing fine and felt grateful that he was smoothly negotiating some of the most inhospitable terrains with ease, and whenever he is in the trough of such blessings, he always gave praises. As he approached a fairly deep corner, parson was ending his prayer when he got into the spirit and started shouting 'praise the lord' repeatedly. The jackass, sighting this as a command to go to a gallop, took off as fast as it could. A very deep precipice was at the corner and the donkey could never negotiate it safely at that speed, but he was responding to commands and he forged ahead.

Parson was still shouting in the spirit when he realized the danger. Suddenly, and not a second too soon, he remembered to shout 'amen' and the jackass came to an abrupt stop only inches from the edge of the precipice. Seeing how closely he had come to his demise, parson in his typical form, delved into prayer again.

And he went into the spirit. The donkey's head was still pointed towards the precipice. Amen!

THE WORM REMEDY

Drinking had become an epidemic in the circuit of churches and pastor decided to spare no effort to convince his congregants of the dangers of alcoholism. Furthermore, it was eating away at his collection proceeds every Sunday. After he had exhausted all the religious and biblical references available in his weekly sermons, pastor decided to cap it all off from a scientific point of view. He did not know that by then, most of his followers were close to giving up this unhealthy lifestyle. He decided on this final Sunday to invite a chemist from the nearby college to do a demonstration. His introduction was brief as he proudly announced that his sermon would be viewed, not spoken.

The esteemed professor was introduced and the congregation watched with delight and admiration as he meticulously turned the entire podium into an impromptu laboratory. Deacon was now the lab assistant. The professor made sure to place all the containers within clear view of the worshippers. After everything was in place, he invited deacon to join him at the podium. He handed deacon a transparent dish that he instructed him to show to everyone. He then pulled out a live and twisting worm from a container. Deacon was told to show the wiggling creature as he had done with the dish. He then directed deacon to place the worm into the empty container, which he did. As the worm wiggled, deacon was asked to open and taste the contents of a bottle that was labeled 'clean water.' When asked what it was, deacon confirmed that it was water. He was then instructed to pour the contents of the bottle into the container with the still wiggling worm. As the water was poured, the worm continued to wiggle and even floated as if it welcomed the hydrating source.

After quite a few seconds of delay, the water was poured from the dish and deacon showed the dish to the congregation. The worm was not only still alive but it was crawling around in the dish.

Deacon was instructed to remove the worm and a new one was placed in the empty dish. That worm was not only bigger but it had more energy than the previous one. The deacon was handed another bottle, this time labeled 'White Rum.' He was instructed to open the bottle and although tempted, decided against tasting its contents, but by then, some members of the congregation confirmed the identity of the liquid with their shouts of 'amen' as the aroma rapidly permeated the building.

During all that time, parson stood with that convincing smirk on his face as he awaited the big bombshell. The great anti climax came, when deacon was instructed to pour the contents of the bottle into the container with the strongly wiggling worm. The liquid did not quite reach the bottom of the container, when the poor vermin desperately lunged forward, spun over on its back, and ceased to move. The shouts from the pastor and the congregation were so loud and prolonged that few people noticed that Sister Ida Lee, a normally quiet and reserved sister, was now jumping and shouting 'hallelujah' at the top of her voice. But parson was one of the few, and he seized the rare opportunity to ask Sister Ida Lee to lead the testimony. Parson could not believe his luck when Sister Lee almost rushed to the microphone.

The shocked congregation fell suddenly silent when they heard this rare voice on the loudspeaker and they listened with great anticipation. In the most eloquent way, Sister Lee addressed the parson, the professor, the deacon and the congregation, and expressed profound gratitude for the blessing she had just received. As everyone listened attentively, parson in particular, Sister Lee went into a litany of experiences she had had with her kids' illnesses over the years. She had been to just about every medical facility until finally, one doctor was able to diagnose the symptoms. But despite the right diagnosis, none of the medications that were prescribed ever worked for her kids, so that is why she was now shouting praises to God for directing the pastor to plan that special service, which has finally led her to find the right remedy to cure her kids of the repugnant worms that have afflicted them for all those years. With that, she stormed out of the church, still shouting hallelujah as the congregation responded with praise the lord. Pastor was confounded but at least he was guaranteed one certain soul.

RIGHTEOUS SCREAMS

The Pentecostal congregation was at its height in praise and the entire church was in motion. There was endless jumping and screaming and some caught in the spirit, were falling on each other. Suddenly, there was a male voice shouting, 'Lord Jesus Christ' repeatedly over all the other voices. Everyone suddenly realized that the voice was no other than that of the notorious praedial thief Zacky, whom the church had targeted for conversion for years. He was now, not only in the church, which is very rare for him, but he was now apparently stung by the holy bug.

As was the custom, the elders rushed to receive the new convert and waited for him to stop screaming and give his testimony. The congregation fell silent as suddenly as the screaming stopped and Zacky was asked to speak. The look of agony was on his face as he started to explain in a still loud, but halting voice, that he was standing by himself, not troubling anyone, when this, (r rated c) woman, jumped right on him and hurt up his sore foot. He had to be quickly ushered out of the church before it became dark.

WHEN THE ROLL IS CALLED UP YONDER

Parson had spent the morning teaching the Sunday school kids songs that required gesticulation. He drilled them in the art of proper interpretation and even reprimanded some of his charges for simple errors they made. During the service he was testing the kids to the delight of the whole congregation. He was especially pleased when Tommy, one of the slower students, correctly pointed up, when he asked him to show where heaven was and down, for hell. He then admonished the congregation to be careful when they gesticulate as they could send the wrong message.

The sermon was a lengthy one and parson was charged in the spirit and gesticulating at will. In closing his sermon, he raised the chorus 'When the roll is called up yonder.' When the chorus was done, he asked the congregants, where they would be when the roll is called up yonder. Not being satisfied with the lackluster response from the worn out audience, he shouted the question a few more times. He was highly charged, when he declared that some in the audience seemed not to be certain where they would be at that time, but he, still shouting, strongly, declared while pointing up; "When the roll is called up yonder." He repeated it a few times, still pointing up "Brothers and sisters, when the roll is called up yonder, I'll be there. I'll be there."

Even Tommy noticed that he was pointing down, deep down, as he repeated the last words.

JUDGMENT DAY

This was not the first time this sailor's ship was docking at this Jamaican port, so he fairy well knew his way around the small town and he even occasionally attended services at this nearby Methodist church, usually when he was bored or drunk. One night he went to service and the topic of the sermon was the judgment day. The parson preached at length about this most eventful day and even questioned the preparedness of his flock. When he gave the graphic description of that day, the sailor could see how the congregation seemed to shudder at the mention of the judgment horn sounding and the fire and brimstone. He also noticed that the parishioners gave generous contributions during the collection.

It so happened that on one of those return visits, the boat was berthed longer than usual and the sailor ran out of spending money and none of his mates had any to lend. Desperation caused him to contemplate some creative means by which he could make some money while on this extended stay, but none seemed plausible. Finally, he decided to visit the church that evening.

But unlike other times, he would be there long before the worshippers gathered for the night service. He was also not dressed in regular clothing, but in a full length, white sailor gown and white sailor pants. He also wore a white headband and he took with him a spare horn from his boat. He did not sit in the pew as usual, but he scouted out the building and selected a strategic spot above the arch that was over the choir and pulpit.

Night came and everyone gathered for service. The time finally came for the collection and parson made the special appeal and reminded the worshippers that the more they give the more they would receive. From his perch, the well garbed intruder could see that the collection plates were specially laden that night He knew why, as the sermon was 'Behold the bridegroom cometh, like a thief in the night' No sooner was the offering blessed and taken and placed in one container in the vestibule, the sailor made his move.

Like he often did on the boat, he raised the huge horn to his mouth, pulled a deep breath and the sound like the judgment horn, pierced the night, deafening every ear within that church. In a matter of seconds that building was empty. No one, not even the parson, was prepared to face the judgment that night, for when he saw that deacon had taken flight and he was left alone, he was overheard saying, "If it's a race, lets have an even start, so I am getting the hell out of here lord."

And with that, he took off and headed for a fence, as the gate was too far away. Unfortunately, as the sailor made his planned exit with the night's proceeds, he happened upon parson, whose jacket tail was caught on the barbed wire fence. On seeing what to him, was a spirit, parson shouted, "Let go of this, (messy stuff), collection money did not buy it." and with that he pulled the coat so hard that half of it was left on the fence, and he took off like a bullet, still swearing to himself.

THE ONE UP ABOVE

The lady of the gentry had a secret life. Her husband worked nights and she led a fairly active nocturnal lifestyle during his absences. On this particular night, visitor number one was right on time, and he was just settling in for his shift when there was a knock on the door. He was trembling in fear of his cover being blown, but the well seasoned two-timer gently showed him a way into the attic to wait out the visit. To the lady's frustration visitor number two, who had a much later appointment, declared that he could not wait that long as he was too desperate to see her again. She tried her best to convince him that his timing was bad and he should leave and return the usual time, as her husband sometimes come home for snack at the end of his first shift.

She did not realize how prophetic she was, as no sooner had she made the utterance, there was another knock on the door and the voice outside was that of her trusting husband. Oddly enough, this was the first time he was ever making an unannounced visit home. Mr. attic dweller, who a few seconds before, was highly hopeful his rival was about to leave as he listened to what transpired between the two people below him, now realized that he was in for the long haul. His anxiety had suddenly reached fever pitch as he was certain that he would soon be having company as he could not think of where his rival would be directed to hide. But as an old artist, the gracious lady delivered, and he overheard the instruction for number two to slip under the bed. Hubby came in and sounded very frustrated, and he desperately needed his wife's support. He was having some serious problems at work and decided to come home to get some comfort and advice before deciding whether to return to work. The lady was at her best as an advisor that night and rightly so.

She succeeded in convincing her frustrated spouse that he should never allow wicked people to cause him to lose his daily bread, so he should return to work. He seemed convinced and was about to leave, when he declared that he needed a white rum to give him a boost. As soon as the first gulp reached his stomach, he seemed to fall into a state of self pity and raised his voice. This caused the roofer, who by then, had fallen asleep, to wake up just in time to hear the husband declare loudly, that only the man up above, (meaning God), knew what he was going through.

Instead of keeping his damn bun-infested mouth shut, mister attic dweller, thinking that the jilted hubby was referring to him, blurted out; "It's not me alone know, the one under the bed know too!"

THE FAMOUS WATER JAR

Across town, another husband also worked nights and wify, dedicated church secretary, loosely socialized with deacon and another brother after hours. This night deacon came early and was about to settle in, when a knock was heard at the door. It was hubby, who had decided to leave work early to surprise his wife that night. Sister looked around for a quick hiding place and decided on a large water jar that stood empty and in plain view in the living room. Anyplace was appropriate for deacon, as long as he could fit. The sister lifted the heavy lid off the jar and deacon wiggled his way in and she quickly placed the lid back on. She went and opened the door and her husband came in. In her nervous state, she did not close the door completely.

She put on a very good show and hubby suspected nothing. But all throughout that time, she was trying to figure a way out for the poor deacon, who was by then in agony, as he baked in the jar. Man and wife were both in the living room, when the door suddenly flew open and in barged Sunday school Superintendent Smith, as if he was 'man-a-yard.' He had thought that the sister had extended a special welcome by leaving the door opened for him.

His belief was suddenly shattered when he found himself facing the man of the house, as he made this awkward, crash entry. Being the actor she was, the wife calmly asked Super, the reason for the rush. He was scanning with both his eyes and his brain for a quick response, when his eyes hit the large water jar, after a quick face gesture from the sister. He suddenly blurted out that parson had sent him to borrow the jar for some church emergency.

Without even a pause, the relieved sister immediately solicited a nod from hubby and the Super headed for the water jar. He lifted that jar so easily, that one would think it was not earthenware, and he strode briskly out of that house. His adrenalin was pumping so hard that he did not feel the dead weight or the muscle pull until he was on top of the hill far away from the rays of the outside lights of the sister's house.

At that point, he carefully helped down the jar, lifted the lid to the sky, and after a very heavy sigh of relief, he emphatically declared "If it wasn't for this jar, what would have happened to us tonight?" He brought his head down just in time to see deacon rise from the jar and exclaimed; "Eeh brother?"

JESUS DIED

On one of his scheduled visits to the church school, rector was quizzing a class on their knowledge of the bible. He came to the story of Jesus and he asked the class to show their hands to answer the question, when did Jesus die. A few kids put up their hands and rector was astonished. But when he got the incorrect responses from the raised hands, his astonishment turned to frustration. How could the senior class not know when Jesus died? Just when he was about to give up, in walked Sister Isabelle's daughter. She was a fixture in church and Sunday school every Sunday. With great expectation, pastor posed the question to his ardent Sunday scholar, only to have her answer 'Christmas day.' Rector was beside himself. He could see with the other kids, they did not attend his church, but Sister Isabelle's daughter? He decided then and there to visit that home to find out what could have gone wrong.

On seeing rector's car approaching her home, Sister Isabelle scurried to straighten up her dilapidated house. By the time rector arrived, the place was relatively neat. But pastor was not his jovial self and the sister noticed that, so she proceeded to ask what the matter was.

Rector painstakingly started to relate the incident at school and then he came to the most devastating part. He told the attentive listeners, who had by then converged in the living room, that when he saw Mary, he was so relieved that she would make him proud and give the correct answer, so he asked her the great question; 'When did Jesus die' and to his disappointment, Mary did not know.

"Him dead Rector?" (Is he dead rector?), came the most stunning response from Sister Isabelle. "I never even hear say him was sick, what kill him?" Rector asked for a drink of water and as he was beating a hasty retreat from the residence, he overheard another member of the household remark, "That's why Rector look so sad." And another pondered; "A wonder when dem a go bury him?"

GIFT OF THE SPIRIT

Sister Jane well knew that parson had a secret passion for the bottle, so on his birthday she made a special cake for him. This was a fruit cake laced with white rum and wine. Parson must have had a field day all week as he seemed to be still slightly high at church that Sunday. During the announcements, he was thanking everyone for making his birthday such a wonderful one. "But last but not least" he said, "I specially want to thank Sister Jane for her lovely present. It was not so much for the gift that was presented, but the spirit in which it was given." And the congregation shouted 'Amen'

LOVE THINE ENEMY

This chronic alcoholic was on the rebound from the disastrous fallout he had suffered from years of indulgence. His attempt at rehabilitation was an uphill climb, marked by relapse after relapse. After deciding that he had had his fill in futility, he went to his favorite bar for an up, close and personal with his demon.

He ordered a White Rum. When he received the drink, he stood up and raised the glass in the air and loudly declared that he was delivering a toast. As the curious patrons fell silent and watched, he spoke up. "You see you rum, yu mek mi lose mi good, good job, you mek mi lose mi beautiful and faithful wife, you mek mi pickney dem shame a mi and abandon mi, and all mi family and friends turn their backs on mi, and mi whole life mash up. So you a mi enemy. But as a Christian, the bible teach mi fi love mi enemy. So mi nah trow yu weh, mi a drink you." And with that he put the glass to his mouth and swallowed every bit.

I'M PREGNANT

The goodly gentleman had visited his doctor for his regular checkup. So as to be routine, the doctor instructed him to return the next day with an overnight sample of his urine for analysis. The gentleman went home and selected a special chimmy, (bedpan), for this collection. In a rather strange development that night, his wife somehow shocked him with some revolutionary ideas about sex. She happened to have attended some women's forum that week and wanted to introduce him to other methods other than the conventional missionary way. He was very reluctant and even questioned his wife's loyalty, but as soon as he relented, he suddenly realized what was missing from his dull life and he threw caution to the wind. He was especially excited with the inversion of the missionary order. After what turned out to be an action-filled night, he woke up and poured his specimen into a bottle and headed for the doctor.

He sat and waited for the urine analysis to be completed. As soon as this was done, the doctor called him in and informed him that his urine showed he was in fine health, except that he was puzzled about something. There was sign of pregnancy in the sample.

The normally calm and dignified gentleman lost his mind and the entire office had to get involved to calm him down. After he kept on repeating "A told her not to do it." (He was referring to the reversed missionary way) "Look what happen to me now! Lord God, what am I going to do?"

After a while, one of the nurses in the office had a hunch and decided to make a call to this irate man's wife at her place of work. The caller returned to the waiting room fighting to hold back laughter, as she whispered something to the doctor, who also struggled to contain himself. The poor patient was once again escorted to a private room and the doctor gave him the good news. Unbeknownst to him, in the excitement of the previous night, his wife had forgotten that he was saving the sample and inadvertently used the night glass, thus contaminating the specimen. He was about to become a proud father; something he had dreamed of for many years. He was hopping, skipping and jumping as he left the doctor's office.

DEADOLOGY

Some stereotypical foreign Adventist theological scholars were on a fact-finding tour of the island as guests of the local fraternity. But they never displayed any goodwill and the local chaperons were getting more and more frustrated with the disrespect that their guests were showing to the locals as they visited the various places on their schedule. On one of these tours, they were at a beach on the north coast, when the foreigners, in their typical fashion, were critical of everyone and everything they saw. They were particularly harsh on the Rastafarians, as in their minds, they were just some silly humans with locks. Although it was not on the schedule, the group decided to charter a boat that was operated by a Rastaman.

The local escorts decided not to go on that boat, so the foreigners boarded and they headed out to sea. They did not reach far before they started to ridicule the subdued Rasta. One asked him if he knew Theology. When he said no, they burst out laughing and told him that if he knew nothing about Theology, half of his life was gone. After they had had their fill of the first joke, another one asked the dread if he knew Biology and the Rasta replied that he did not know those sums. That made them laugh the more. They were having the time of their lives. The Rastaman was getting agitated, but he only answered in the negative as the 'ologies' were thrown at him by his elated passengers.

They were way out at sea, when a huge wave hit the boat and the fragile vessel took in a lot of water and started to lisp. Instead of turning back, the Rasta was still heading out to sea. The boat was filling up and the passengers were now showing signs of nervousness, but the Rastaman did not flinch. When it appeared that the boat was almost half-way full, the Rasta turned to the, by now silent, trembling, half wet scholars and asked, "Do you know Swimmology?" "What is that? We have never heard of it," one scholar nervously remarked. "Well, if you don't know Swimmology, I am afraid, the whole of you life gone. As you can see, the boat is sinking and I and I know Swimmology so I and I will be leaving you to Deadology." With that he dived off the boat. Luckily a passing boat rescued the visitors, and from that day they were the best guests the local hosts could have had around.

LIGHT ONE FIMMI

A poor wonderer decided to make this cave, by a lonely roadside, his home. This was fairly close to a little community in Portland. It did not take long before he became a fixture in the communities around and he was helpful and friendly to just about everyone; who reciprocated in kind

In the wee hours one morning, he was awakened by a loud explosion that came from a car that had just blown a tire right in front of his cave. As he crawled out carefully to see more, he overheard the driver swearing and saw him walk angrily towards the mouth of the cave.

The driver leaned against the wall and took out a cigarette and lit up to clear his head. As soon as he did so, out of nowhere came a voice "Light up one deh fi mi to."

Without a second thought, the stranded driver was off like Bolt, leaving even his lit cigarette behind. The cave dweller retrieved it quickly. After a while a car pulled up and a familiar voice called out to Mr. Cave Dweller, who happily came down to help the stranded motorist. The terrified motorist had just rushed to his friend's house for rescue, after he was certain a ghost had just asked him for a cigarette.

JAH PORTRAIT

A thunder storm was in progress and all the patrons at this wayside bar and restaurant in Clarendon, had taken shelter indoors. The lightning was intense and the thunder loud. To the amazement of those assembled, a Rastaman was spotted outside, close to a clump of trees, making movements as if posing for a camera. At each lightning flash, the dread would change pose as he rotated. He even brushed his locks and smiled in the process. A very concerned member of the group called out to the dread and asked him if he did not know the lightning could strike him. The dread looked towards the man and asked him which lightning. When the patron responded, the dread told him he had got it all wrong; the flashes were from Jah's flash camera and Jah was taking his photograph. He continued to pose until one burst of lightning struck a nearby tree sending off sparks that singed some of the dread's locks. On feeling the heat, the dread flew into the building shouting, "Jah dread I!"

YOU OR YOU

During the Jamaica Omnibus era, any bus starting with the number three held the reputation of carrying the hottest chicks from the hills of Saint Andrew to the city of Kingston on a daily basis. But it was also from this area that a lot of Rastafarians made their daily trek to the capitol as well, and so the occasional conflict between Beauty and the Dread could never be avoided. The dreads never passed up an opportunity to agitate and embarrass, whom they saw as, the hoity toity socialites. But the mostly brownings were not totally helpless; they retaliated most of the times. On one of those mornings, this dread was alone at the bus stop when two of these chicks joined him. His efforts to make small talk were totally ignored and he was angry, so he came up with a plan. He knew that those St Andrews ladies mostly sat in the rear of the buses to avoid the crowd, so he headed straight to the extreme rare ahead of the pair. The bus was filling up, so they all sat in the long rear seat, but the duo made sure to put some distance between themselves and the Rastaman.

The bus had stopped at a red light and during that silence, the dread pulled up closely to the unsuspecting pair and let off a loud gaseous explosion. As the shocked passengers looked back to where the sound originated, the dread, with a look of scorn on his face, pointed to the imprisoned duo and declared, "If it's not you, it's you." When the laughter erupted, all the poor ladies could do was try futilely to deny the claim, but they were drowned out by the laughter. In their rage, they tried to think of a way to get back at the dread before they reached their destination and a glorious opportunity came when they spotted a bed bug crawling on the dread's shirt.

One of the young ladies used her fingernails to pick the bug from the dread's shirt and held it up and called out for everyone to look what she found on the dread. Everyone looked around just in time to see when the dread grab something from the young lady's hand and shouted "Gimmi back this dirt; everything you girls see the dread have you want to take it away." The poor duo was once again the brunt of the joke, as no one had seen what was really dragged from that hand.

THE COFFIN RIDE

A truck was on its way from Spanish Town to deliver an empty coffin somewhere in Manchester. A sideman was on the truck and somewhere near Old Harbor, it began to rain. There was no more room in the cab for an extra passenger. The creative sideman came up with the brilliant, yet spooky, idea, to board the empty coffin to avoid getting drenched.

A little way out of May Pen, a hitchhiker flagged down the truck and the considerate driver saw that he was already soaking wet, so the open truck would not matter. The hitchhiker was more than grateful for the ride and hopped in quickly. His delight was short lived however, when he realized that he would be sharing the rear with a coffin. He pulled back to the tailgate of the truck and did not for one moment take his eyes off that coffin.

The truck was approaching Porus, when it stopped raining. The newcomer was still holding a stare at the coffin when to his horror, the lid opened and the head of a man appeared, enquiring if it had stopped raining. Without a moment's, hesitation, that poor guy just stepped backwards off the speeding truck.

MIDNIGHT DATE

R.B from May Pen worked nights at Alpart Bauxite Plant, near Mandeville. His shift usually ended at midnight and he commuted daily. He was the consummate womanizer and made no qualms about it. In the wee hours one morning, he was on his way home on a familiar street in Mandeville, when his well tuned Ford Cortina GT's engine suddenly went dead. As a fairly good mechanic, he checked everything out, but could not diagnose the problem.

Just when he was about to walk to some friend's home for help, who could appear from out of nowhere, but a stunning chick, whom he would occasionally see but never got a chance to talk to. She was standing at a nearby gate as if waiting for some one. He could never believe his luck and made no hesitation to invite her over to where his car was. He started some small talk, but only got smiles and nods in response. He however opened his passenger door and invited the young lady inside and she willingly complied. The door was closed and he got comfortable just chatting away. The responses were still nods, smiles and an occasional grunt, but he was so smitten he didn't see anything wrong with that.

As was his typical habit, he decided to go straight to point zero with his hand, before even a hug or a kiss. As soon as his hand reached to where point zero should have been, instead of feeling flesh under skirt, he only saw a big puff of smoke and his seat was empty and the door never opened.

Within minutes, he collapsed on his verandah in May Pen, dozens of miles away, not being able to recall his passage through

Williams Field, Porus or Toll Gate. Neither could he remember how the stranded car managed to start.

After many days, he mustered enough courage to relate the incidence to his coworkers, only to discover that he was just one of the many who had been jilted by this sexy engine jamming entity. They all had seen her around, truly alive, but never connected. Apparently in life, she had similar crushes too but was unable to act out her fantasies until her death from child's birth. From that day, RB. pledged, that he would never again trust any female shadow, after dark.

COUGH OUT THAT LASS

Mr. Chin had an endowment problem, but he kept up a facade for years to make himself look super. Things eventually caught up with him when his latest quarry, a super hot momma, got bored with the charade, even though the financial incentives were great. During action times, she would just cough and Mr. Chin would be expelled. Whether it was out of love, pride, or both, Mr. Chin decided to stop at nothing to save this relationship.

He approached a body builder friend whom he knew to be at the top of his game and offered to engage his services to help him save this relationship. The plan was that macho man would be in a closet next to the bed and Mr. Chin would start his fore activities like he did every night, and then a quick switch would be made That part of the exercise was always exhilarating to momma and Mr. Chin was good at that, so when he excused himself in the midst of the session, she thought he had some new plans to boost his performance for the next phase. And he did. For no sooner had he returned it was like he had morphed into a beast and momma was blown away, her voice now at decibels unheard of before.

Mr. Chin, now crouched down where macho man had been, started to catch the rhythm and counting strokes. In his excitement he was like a jockey flashing his whip at every sound. But at one point the sound was reaching a crescendo and Mr. Chin got carried away. He was straining hard to keep quiet but could contain himself no more, when a melodious sound floored him. Instead of keeping his overcharged mouth shut, Mr. Chin blurted out. "Yes! I want you to cough out that lass, (rated r), now, cough out that lass!"

PAJAMA SLEEP OVER

Brother man had a strong crush on attractive church sister, so he visited often to chase the scriptures. On one of his visits it started to rain and brother was glad that he had a legitimate excuse to hang around. Every now and then there was a lull in the showers and brother pretended to try to leave, but was glad when sister advised him to wait as the rains would soon cease altogether and he could go home. But to brother's secret delight, the rain fell right into the night and he was pleasantly stuck. It was getting late and sister wanted to go to bed. Sister was very concerned for the brother's predicament and expressed regret that he did not have a pair of pajamas. If he did, she eventually told him, she would allow him to stay. She could not understand why the brother suddenly disappeared, but she had thought that he was in the bathroom. To her surprise, who could come through her front door wet as a chicken, and displaying a dry pair of pajamas in a plastic bag?, no other than the brother.

His plan backfired that night as the sister and all of us consider him silly, and we support the dispatch of his wet behind home. But he just did not think that was fair. He had his pajamas and it was still raining. You be the judge

NOT MY HOME

Very striking beauty flagged down this cab in Half Way Tree one late afternoon and when the cab pulled over, she opened the door and sat in the back. She seemed to be slightly perturbed and all that she said to the driver was, "Take me home please!" The friendly cabbie was about to move off, when he turned and politely asked, "And where is home, my good lady?" To his amazement her reply was, "I'm sorry, but I don't give strangers my address." She was really perturbed.

AN ENIGMA

He is the most vilified character in the Jamaican male psyche and no ghost; not even coolie duppy, elicit such dread among male spouses, like this phantom. He is not in the least omnipotent, in fact, he is anything but. He is not omniscient either, as he is very fallible and sometimes gets caught. But even when he is caught, he still remains a mystery. But his greatest attribute is his omnipresence. He can be many places at the same time. Even some, who are terrified by him, could themselves be him at one time or the other, so he has little or no real identity. But the pain he exacts on his hapless victims can be excruciating and often leads to homicide, suicide or both. To joke to anyone that this menace is at his house, is to do it at your own peril, as no one finds this amusing. I had a firsthand experience of this phenomenon at a favorite hangout in Port Maria one evening, when a well respected professional, yawned loudly after consuming several strong ones. A so-called friend of his, himself inebriated by the indulgence, loudly declared that the yawn was a sure indicator that this nemesis was at his home. That gentleman became so enraged that he instantly stormed out of that bar, not even saying goodbye to anyone and even forgot to pay his bill, but as he was a regular, the bartender did not have to worry. But his action obviously confirmed the worst and we all shared his pain.

Following his departure, we all engaged in a crash course in discretion, when anyone in our midst, in the future, yawns. As I write, I know there art hundreds of Jamaican males who are yawning now as their homes are being violated, or their properties are being defiled by this diabolic predator. And if you did not know his name, you will still feel his impact.

Yours truly,
Joseph Grinder.

BOOT PRINTS IN THE SAND

The farmers in the close-knit community in Saint Catherine could not understand why they were losing their cattle at nights, and no one had a clue as to who was doing it. They would wake up in the mornings and their animals would be gone without a trace. They were certain no vehicle had taken their cows out of the district, as they started to block the roads and even monitor them at nights. Finally, they thought they had a breakthrough one morning, after it had rained the night before. They were able to track footprints of some cattle to the side of the river that ran through the community. There were also water boot prints amongst those of the cattle's. They were certain they were on to something and crossed to the other side to continue the tracking, as that was the only way out of the district. They were in for a disappointment when their search turned up only water boot prints on the other side of the river. The cows did not cross the river, maybe the prints were made long ago and the rains just highlighted them.

But the cow stealing persisted and the farmers, along with the local police, were at their wit's end. It rained again one night when another farmer lost his prized bull, along with some heifers. The next morning some one reported that they heard sounds like an animal in distress, coming from the river. On their way to the river, the searchers saw fresh tracks and followed them until they came to the edge, where they found the lost bull, stuck, belly deep, in the swollen waters. They all joined forces and succeeded to dislodge the animal from its watery trap.

But they had another surprise coming. As the animal was being lifted, the men holding the feet all declared that they felt rubber.

When the animal was raised, four water boots fell off its feet. Then and there, the mystery of the disappearing cow tracks was solved, and it did not take long for them to use the water boot tracks to lead them to a neighboring district. There some stolen cows were found with a butcher, who actually supplied the same district with meat every Friday.

SUICIDE BACKUP PLAN

Depressed young man thought he had had enough of a bad life and decided to end it all by hanging himself He wanted to make the process as fool proof as ever, so he chose a tree limb that hung over a deep blue hole in this wide river. He could not swim so he figured if the limb broke he had the contingency plan to drown instead. His plans were going smoothly and the rope was fastened to the tree limb in no time. The rope was then attached to his neck and he whispered a final prayer and asked God to forgive him. It was then time to make the leap, and he did it with reckless abandon.

As the strain reached the rope and the sting of death hit the falling man, the limb broke under the stress and the young man fell into the deep blue hole. Without even realizing it, that frightened youngster made a desperate dash for the shore and reached it in record time, even with the large limb and rope in toe. It was only when he heard himself say "My God, if I could not swim, look what would happen to me?" did he remember that before that event, he would have drowned in a tea cup. Needless to say, he lived happily ever after and even became a life guard part time.

HOLD THE LIGHT OFFICER

Parade was a great meeting place from in the Colonial era and even international conferences were held there. But as was always the case, it was the haven for pickpockets and every type of opportunistic small time hoodlums. After receiving one report too many, of motor vehicles being vandalized or broken into, the police stepped up their patrols, especially during conferences. It was during one of these conferences that a patrolling officer came upon a man removing a tire from what seemed like a disabled car. When he approached the vehicle the tire remover expressed joy at the approach of the officer and asked him kindly to help him with some light. The officer was glad to oblige so he stayed with the stranger and held his flashlight until the tire was removed and the motorist thanked him graciously and rolled the tire away as the officer continued his patrol.

The conference ended and the parking lot was emptying. But a report suddenly swirled, that quite a few cars were vandalized. The officers were all involved in the investigations, when our helpful cop came upon the said car from which the tire was taken as he held his flashlight earlier. But instead of a young well spoken Kingstonian, the man who declared ownership, and held the key, was a German diplomat. Imagine how stupid that poor cop felt when he was forced to admit that he was conned by the quick-witted crook as he willingly held the lights as the tire was being stolen.

NARWAJI, THE GREAT

He was one of the most feared obeah men in St Mary and he also had a mean streak when it came to women. It was said that he would blame and beat his spouses for any misfortune he experienced, like at one time, he came home from a pilgrimage only to find his entire field of bananas blown down. A storm had passed through in his absence and despite the fact that all the neighboring farms were affected; he gave his St Elizabeth woman a beating, claiming she was the one who pushed the trees down. He was a resourceful obeah man so he did not wait for the jobs to come to him, he along with his trusted henchmen, created the jobs. Whenever business was slow, all he needed was a superstitious target. In this case he found the ideal one in Jefferies Town

She may have been to him before, but he knew that she had some means. Without warning, stones started falling on this lady's house at nights. Immediately, she went to the cops who paid a visit in broad daylight, only to find her claim spurious as there were no stones lying around in her flat front yard, and she had claimed that everyone in the house heard lots of stone fall in the front yard. She even dared to invite the cops to pay a night visit to witness the phenomena first hand, but those cops seemed so scared of their very shadow in the day, who could even think that they would dare a night visit? But they actually tried, but as the sound of the first volley hit the roof that night, the lawmen took off so fast it was only when they had returned to the station did they remember they had actually left a jeep parked at the spooky site. The haunted victim was already leaning towards the supernatural, as she was puzzled by the absence of the stones.

Where were the stones? She had to walk. (Seek out an obeah man) and Narwaji was consulted.

He paid her a visit and after a lot of crazy antics, he promised to spend the might outside her home. Remarkably, no stones fell on the property for the entire night as he had told his cronies not to pack any missiles until further instructed. He attributed the cessation of the stoning to a dialogue he had had with the spirits, but he indicated they were angry and had to be appeased. He told her that some envious neighbor of hers had set the spirits and they actually operated from the nearby cemetery. He recommended a goat sacrifice and feast and told her his fee for the job. She at first decided not to accept the proposal but the following night the bombardment resumed with more intensity than before. There were so many missiles thrown that night that, if the residents had gotten the courage to go out early that morning, they would have seen some of the pieces still not totally melted. But with the night's intensity no one dared to go out early.

As early as she could, she visited Norwaji. She handed him his fees, and the feast was planned for the following night, followed by the séance around midnight at her house. A fairly large crowd had gathered, some associates of Narwaji and the victim, and supporters from her church and the community. The large ram goat was sacrificed and as the feast was being prepared there was a lot of chanting, singing, praying and turn-the-roll, dancing. As soon as the feast was near over, Narwaji called everyone to attention. He declared that the moment had come for the great miracle and that every one should join him in a march to the cemetery. He raised a full plate of food and declared that the spirit had to be fed before the final ritual could commence.

They all marched to the gate of the cemetery, where they were told to gather. The nervous group watched as Norwaji raised the dish in the air and disappeared into the pitch darkness of the cemetery. Minutes later, he emerged, his face all white and he looked like the dead. His disciples were now shouting louder and dancing more rigidly. The momentum was now heading for a fever pitch and again Norwaji hushed the crowd and shouted that the time of liberation had come and he raised the tune, 'The lion of Judah shall break every chain'. Every one joined in vigorously as he jumped and railed. He called out, what he said was, the name of the spirit and by then everyone seemed caught up in the fever. "Come forth!" he ordered, raising both hands as he faced the cemetery gate. As the, by now, traumatized assembly looked on, he announced that the spirit was commandeered and was on its way out of the cemetery. He then turned to the group and asked if they wanted to see the real ghost as it made its exit, to which those who could, shouted 'yes.' Suddenly, what looked like a fast moving cloud appeared out of the darkness and as it broached the dim light, a white flash appeared and disappeared faster than the eyes could discern. And there was the sound of a plate falling, but by then, most of those present had fainted at the sight of the ghost and Narwaji quickly retrieved the plate that had accidentally fallen from his crony; the said plate he had taken into the cemetery to feed the ghost, who also doubled as the ice thrower. He loudly and quickly declared the session over and melted into the darkness as those left standing, attend to the fallen

The following night was the most peaceful at that haunted house and Narwaji's fame spread.

I AM HOLDING A BATTERY

Motorist was very frustrated, as his day was not going too well, and to add insult to injury, his early morning trip to Ocho Rios was interrupted by a flat tire. He had his hood up to warn approaching traffic to take caution and was so pre-occupied with removing his tire that he paid little attention, if any, to a car that had stopped in front of his. He was very relieved when he finally got the rear tire off and got up to put it in his trunk. But as he was doing so, he heard, what sounded like someone using some sort of tool to pull something in the front of his car, so he hurried to see what was going on. He arrived just in time to see this man, the apparent driver of the stopped car, marching away clasping a battery in his hands. A quick glance confirmed that his battery was missing. He angrily asked the vandal what was really going on, to which he casually replied, and I quote "I see you taking a tire; I am just holding a battery." And he did not willingly give up his loot.

BANANA STALK

The Land Authority in Saint Mary had undertaken a massive agricultural development project to help small farmers increase production of food crops after bad weather had devastated their farms. Farmers were free to choose any crop that they decided could be produced viably on their land and the government would provide technical assistance along with up front cash for the preparation of land and purchase of planting material and fertilizer.

In one old farming community in the parish, the farmers were very grateful for the assistance and the extension officers were impressed with their responses. But there was one particular farmer who stood out above the rest. He had earmarked a large portion of his property for banana production and was the first to do clearing and plowing. As soon as he received his portion of money he went straight ahead and planted his entire field with banana suckers. When the field officers visited, they were proud to see the beautiful layout of the banana field as the seedlings laid neatly in line as they had instructed. They decided to adopt this particular farm as their pilot project and planned to hold by-weekly demonstrations there.

But after the second month, everyone noticed that there were just a few young shoots rising out of the ground. In comparison, all the other banana farmers had beautiful young shoots all over their land. Near the middle of the third month, when everyone assembled for the field day, they received a message that the host farmer would not be present that day. They still proceeded with the training which started with a question and answer period.

One lifelong farmer, who seemed almost fatigued, got up and questioned why there were so few young shoots visible on this plot, when all of his were over a foot tall and the host farmers' were planted long before. That seemed to have gotten everyone's attention. But even before anyone could speak again, another farmer wanted to know where the host farmer could have gotten such a large amount of seedlings in such short a time while he had been waiting for weeks for a delivery from Portland.

On a hunch, one of the officers decided to inspect the projecting stalks more closely. As he pulled one piece, it came right up and there was nothing left in the ground. All that there was, was a six inch piece of banana stalk. Everyone joined in the search only to find that the few seedlings that were planted were the few that were seen growing out of the ground. All the rest of the holes contained only tree trunks that were craftily chopped into pieces and placed in the ground in a bid to convince the officers. The cunning farmer had received his full payoff but did not produce anything more than a scam to get free government money.

THE MECHANIC

He was known as a Volkswagen specialist and he was one of the best mechanics I have known. But he had a unique disposition. He had left Sinclair's Auto Repairs in Ocho Rios for what, I think, was his love of the bottle, and he worked from home. His former clients from Sinclair followed him home and really saved a lot on car repairs. But there was one snag; the early bird catches the worm. If you were the first client to reach his gate, make sure that you come armed, not so much with money for the job or car parts, but a flask of White Rum. I learnt the hard way one morning, when I arrived first at his gate. As I waited for him to wake up, another car arrived and the driver went straight to his door and handed him a small flask, and in no time he was out looking at his car as I protested. He hardly seemed to care, as he had already consumed most of the contents of that bottle. In no time that guy was on his way home. But before he left, he let me in on the secret. From then on, I was the early bird with the rum. I was also told that he would be very unwilling to work for anyone who did not supply the wake-me-upper. If you were among the first three to arrive, there was a good chance your job would be done that same day, but as the day progressed, he slowed as the rum set in and he would just disappear without any notice, and that was it for the day.

When I questioned the patience of some of these clients, they told me horror stories. The most memorable of all, was that of a fairly well established area mechanic who left numerous nuts and bolts strewed around a gentleman's car, when he came to pick it up after a major job. When he asked the mechanic about the screws, his response was that the Germans were over generous with their use of bolts and nuts, many of which were not really necessary, as his car would run well without them. Wisely, the owner decided to pick up the screws and take the car to another place where the mechanics expressed surprise that his car never fell apart on its way to them.

THE SHOE DEAL

Country man went to town to do his once a year shopping. He was a stingy guy who never passed up a good deal. He was at the Pink and Black store downtown, when he ran into some shoes that really caught his eyes. His foot size was eight and he found the perfect fit in various colors. He still tried to negotiate a discount but was told that that was the rock bottom price.

Country man looked upon the shelf and noticed that the number twelve sizes were also priced the same as the number eights. He was sure that that was a mistake and quickly bought two pairs. He made a hasty exit from the store before anyone could discover the error, he surmised. It was only when he reached home and was still gloating about his luck and great skills at bargaining, that someone pointed out his silliness, and the receipt said no refunds and no returns.

TALL TALES

I could not hear them often enough, especially when it rained and I was holed up in some makeshift shelter, in the grateful company of any male senior citizen, who would be meticulously building his cigar from scratch, as he delved into the bizarre. I could never say that those elders expected me to believe that their grandfathers had guns that could shoot around corners or that the mosquitoes in the woods bordering the parishes of Saint Mary and Saint Ann, were so huge that one was seen using a cow's horn to pick his teeth. But looking back at the tale of the guns, it seems they were onto something, as the cruise missile seemed to have had a precursor What was most interesting was that those elders never left themselves out of the drama. They always gave themselves a starring role in some and they always swore on their tobacco pipes that they were true. And if you dare try to question the time of those occurrences or their birth, they would tell you that everything happened in the era 'when salt fish a shingle house,' or before 'Whoppy kill Fillup'. But the more of the elders you encountered, the more the versions changed. But it did not matter who told my favorite one, I was always mesmerized by it.

He, whoever was telling the tale, had farmed way up in some mountains, decades before and had kept a gourd full of water hanging from an Acacia tree near the hut in his field. He was suddenly recruited to join the military and dispatched to England to fight in one of the world wars. On his return, he decided to resume farming right where he left off. Everywhere was fully overgrown but there were some indigenous plants that still stood their grounds against the wild vegetation He decided to go over to where the hut had been in a bid to rebuild it. As he approached the area, he noticed that the Acacia tree was still alive. But as he looked up, something caught his eyes. Right at the spot from where the gourd usually hung, he noticed that the gourd had rotted away completely but mysteriously, it left the water still hanging in the same shape of the gourd. He never had to worry about thirst.

Implausible? Only in the tropics. In snowy regions water hangs, but in the form of ice. An old acquaintance of mine told me that when he lived in upstate New York one of his winter pastimes was to go outside his home during some cold mornings and urinate, just to watch the liquid become a line of ice before it hit the ground. And that reminds me of my farm worker relative who told me that one day it was so cold in Canada that he and his neighbor greeted each other, but the words froze and they had to go inside in the warmth, before the words defrosted and they could hear what each other had said.

NARROW ROADS + IMPATIENCE = DRAMA

The episodes have no end, from Flat Bridge to The Junction Road in Saint Mary and beyond. Every curvy, steep or narrow bit of roadway has a story. The Flat Bridge drama is about two aristocrats who happened to have the misfortune of arriving at the famous bridge from opposite directions at exactly the same time. They were both in cars that did not leave much space for other road users, let alone pass each other on this precarious bit of history. Each had slightly entered the bridge from his side and the typical stand off commenced. At first, they stared each other down but nothing happened. By then other motorists happened upon the scene and seeing the type of cars involved, saw an opportunity to witness a live display of the rich and famous in their moments of compromise.

As the expectant onlookers waited, they noticed that one of the drivers took out a newspaper and in clear view of the other, raised his feet to his dash, opened the paper and started to read as if he was in his living room. The other driver looked uncharacteristically calm to the disappointment of the spectators. The studious motorist was reading for a while, when his rival called a bystander and asked him to deliver a message for him. The messenger went over to the laid back driver and, like he was instructed, politely expressed greetings from the other and mentioned how much it seemed he was enjoying the morning news. He was sorry to interrupt him but, if he did not mind, he would be grateful if, after he finished reading, he could send the paper over so that he could catch up on the latest happenings too.

The reader was so taken off guard that without another second's delay, he put his car in reverse and even smiled as he waved to the witty driver as he exited the bridge on his way to Kingston; talk of defusing a potential explosion. "Were those the good old days or what?"

LOOK OUT FOR CARS

The wife was sitting in the front passenger seat from where she could see the approaching traffic. Because the driver-husband was on the blind side, he asked her to look to see if any 'car' was approaching, so he could decide when to go. She looked and told him no, so he made his turn only to be slammed broadside by a pickup truck. Although they survived without serious injury, the husband was furious and scolded his frightened wife for causing the accident. He asked her if she did not see the pickup coming and she replied yes. When he asked her why she did not tell him, she told him that he had said she should look to see if any 'car' was coming. And no car was coming.

MOVE THE ACCIDENT PLEASE

The two cars collided on Marescaux Road just east of Crossroads. The traffic cop was in the process of preparing the report, when he ran into a roadblock; neither he nor anyone nearby could spell the name of the street. He became really angry and asked the parties why they had to crash on a street that was so hard to spell. His insistence that the parties move the accident to Slipe Road, an easier street to spell, and parallel a block away, could only be thwarted by one driver's agility to sprint to the next intersection where he got the spelling right.

SUCH AN INSULT

The semi-illiterate, but very proud farmer, found himself with his back against the wall, in a bar in Yallahs one afternoon. Someone had asked him to spell the word mosquito. He rose and strongly declared that he was insulted, for if someone intended to ask him to spell an animal, at least let it be a more formidable and larger one, which should be much harder to spell; like a cow, not a tiny mosquito. And with that he stormed out of the bar.

THE JUNCTION ROAD IN ST. MARY

This roadway is so extremely curvy and narrow that motorists using that thoroughfare would carry a designated person who would act as a forerunner. At the approach to the most dangerous curves, the driver would pull over and let this individual run ahead and look if any vehicle was approaching from the opposite direction. If no vehicle was approaching, he would sprint back and board the vehicle before the situation changed. Most times it worked well, but there were occasions when the sprinter was either not fast enough or the next car was approaching at a high rate of speed, and that was when things really got ugly. You would wonder why the forerunner did not just call the driver forward instead of sprinting back, but the explanation was that if there was hardly enough space for the two vehicles to pass on the short straight-aways, how much more dangerous it would be if a door was opened at the deep narrow curves

PEOPLE OF THE CLOTH

A surprisingly large percentage of Jamaicans, mostly male, are people of the 'cloth.' And my euphemism is deliberate; I mean 'claut;' the most common ingredient in the profanity cook book. I could think of no other nation on earth that could dare compete with that tropical paradise in the sport of obscene expressions. Take for example, the United States, the greatest nation of modern times, has unbelievably, only one bad word. That poor word is so overused that it could claim verbal harassment and abuse. There are hardly more than three contexts in which it could be expanded. Compare that to its Jamaican counterparts that form part of an unwritten encyclopedia. I have known Jamaicans who could complete more than one sentence, sterile free. There were some I heard of, who would swear until the nearby surroundings become dark. There were even some who could attract lightening when they went berserk. And of course I know one individual who could do all the above and more, and he lived in the area where I grew up and attended school. He also drove a beautiful truck.

We called him Bad word. His family was one of the most exemplary I have known and his kids were saintly. How else could they have been? How many bad words could any one residence take? As even one more from any other family member, could have caused a super saturation which could literally result in a methane type explosion.

He drove his truck to our co-operative farm to transport citrus one early morning, just like he had done numerous times before. Only this time, someone must have ticked him off en-route and he was on edge. I have heard him in his element before, but never on the farm as he showed restraint, usually; when he knew the farm officials were within earshot. And when I say earshot I mean up to a mile away as his range was long. He especially respected the overseer. But on this morning in question, he defied the odds. I can honestly say that some of the loaders seemed bored and wanted some entertainment. So when he tried to tell them to speed up, I remember one in the group, who I knew as a very righteous gentleman, proceeded to mock him in response and that was when he exploded.

We were just a few hundred yards from the overseer's house and he was home. The fiery sparks engulfed the entire valley, sending echoes against echo as the sounds ricocheted off the steep hills and precipices nearby. A glance at the performer revealed froth oozing from both corners of his mouth. He paused only to catch his breath and in the silence, the earth seemed to tremble in anticipation of another blast. By then the loaders seemed subdued, just doing their work and no one was even smiling. They had got more than they bargained for. The ever tranquil and sacred homestead was now being desecrated and they could do nothing about it. But suddenly their hopes were revived as out of nowhere, a familiar voice sounded from the gates of the great house and the image of the overseer appeared, strolling down the hill towards us. As soon as he saw the overseer, Bad Word fell silent as he approached the truck. The overseer obviously pretended he never heard a sound but he had made sure to clean his throat as if to warn of his approach He knew everyone would be civil and that includes Bad word.

As he approached the group, he said a big good morning to everyone, but before he could say anything more, Bad Word interrupted and in the most humble and contrite manner, proceeded to apologize for his disgraceful behavior as he was not aware he was home. But he assured him that that would never happen again. The overseer was obviously flattered and turned and started to leave, but Bad Word was not done yet. It appeared he thought that his apology was not enough. "Mass Ali," he said,

"I am really sorry for my bad behavior. I came here this morning in a good mood, but;" he raised his voice; "you have some (r, rated c, unlimited) man on this (b, rated c, unlimited) farm, etc." The busher beat a hasty retreat, as no one could control the laughter, and that angered Bad Word even the more. He never stopped until it appeared he ran out of oxygen.

NO JOKING MATTER

I watch millions of Americans line up, like sheep to the slaughter, to receive the so-called HINI vaccine and it looks ominous to me. Where did this virus come from? Always somewhere else, like Aids. Aids purportedly came from Africa because of interaction with some little green monkeys. But it did not kill anyone on the continent from creation, until it mysteriously arrived in North America, where it practiced on Americans and was so successful that it did not only spread over the western world, but it got enough expertise to go back across the oceans, ambushed the bush doctors and, with vengeance, ravaged the cradle of civilization. I also believe the swine flu was said to have had its origin there too and then there was the bird flu.

All that hoop-la about bird flu, I believe, was not necessary, as I could remember growing up in rural Jamaica where every now and then, strange viruses would cause us to lose some of our farmyard animals, especially chickens, and we would bury the fallen and in no time the stock would be replenished, sometimes augmented by a few heads from a neighboring district. But one thing I well remember, no human was ever in jeopardy or ever became ill with these animals, so there was no need for panic.

How could these modern-day viruses spread all over the world in such a short time? Airways, and possibly, direct passenger delivery? Who knows? But one thing I am led to believe; there is a conspiracy. The plagues of ancient times spread logically to neighboring countries and trade or military routes. I know airlines travel the world but what are the chances that every airline would have at least one passenger that could infect up to millions in some countries, and especially with a virus like HIV, that is mainly spread through direct sexual intercourse or blood transfusion. There would have had to be a hell-of-a-lot of sex going on. The biblical account of the plagues of Pharaoh's Egypt made no mention of them spreading beyond its borders. The only similarity with the modern day viruses and those of ancient times, like the Athenian and Bubonic plagues, was the source of their origin; Africa again. I honestly do not know why I have developed such strong misgivings about these new epidemics, but I predict massive fallout in the near future. It is surely profitable to have the entire world as a client. This is no joking matter. Prepare for the next epidemiological windfall.

PERSPECTIVE ON LIFE (1)

It's not so much on life, but death. Why are we so afraid of it, especially when we all will face it eventually? I know it mostly has to do with our fear of the unknown and death itself is at times, preceded by painful experiences. In death, we change our form from the vulnerable mortal to the invincible immortal. If death is that bad, how comes no one ever returned from it, even though he or she has the supernatural power to do so? Don't tell me about ghosts now.

It could well be that when you die the new experience is such, that you would never trade it for the old earth experience, and you do not anymore worry for your loved ones left behind. You can't wait for them to get the surprise of their 'lives,' rather, 'deaths', when they arrive in the great beyond to realize that earth is the only hell there is. Who would want to go back there?

AND ON HELL

If I am to interpret the scriptures correctly, eternity follows death, no matter to where; Heaven or Hell. Heaven will be full of milk and honey. That may seem attractive to some starving folk, but I drink milk with caution and I am not lactose intolerant. Honey, on the other hand, is absolutely cloying, and would the bees surrender their bounty without rendering righteous stings? And how boring could it be for the saints to just laze around in Paradise? I understand the desperation of King James to rationalize the unknown, but he has certainly left me thinking for a long time.

His theory on Hell beats all. It will be a place of eternal flames, so before I even try to think about it, I will seek refuge with the Jehovah's Witnesses, as they graciously demand an answer to the following question; 'What would the Great Creator stand to gain from watching his glorious or inglorious creation barbequed forever?' How much heat can a man take? One thing I have gotten to know about all of God's created animals is their amazing ability to adopt and even evolve. Give them a few decades anywhere and they will develop some means of survival, especially if they are natty dreads. How can a human burn for a thousand years and not figure a way out? And if he could tolerate the flames, then he would definitely be coping all right. And what sin would he have to commit to warrant such punishment? I am not forgetting that even one sin is a disqualifier for the Promised Land. The Creator seemed to have gotten a bad rap from King James, but fortunately for him, the Jehovah's Witnesses manage to counter, by theorizing that The Almighty would see no pleasure in destroying his great creation; he will only revamp this earth.

But I close by declaring that there are really some human I know, who could well do with some incineration. I will not name any names, but you damn well know some of the types I am talking about

(2)

Behavioral scientists, who usually have nothing to do, but are well paid in the non-process, will spend a lot of time researching which foot of shoes a person usually puts on first or which socks. Finally I have found a major challenge for them. "Gentlemen," as I am certain no woman would waste time to become behavioral. (I may be wrong) "Kindly research why I wake up early every morning except when I should, and why do I have no toothache on the morning I should see the dentist? Why do the checks never come in the mail on the day I need them?" These are just a few to start with and I know they will take you forever as you have not solved the chicken or the egg controversy yet. And by the way, was Murphy, the law guy, a lawyer, politician, behavioral scientist or all of the above?

AND ON GOVERNANCE AND POLITICS

Over the years the world has been fed the myth that capitalism and democracy are compatible. This could not be any further from the truth. In fact, both of them are on a collision course that will culminate with a catastrophic occurrence, tantamount to Armageddon. Let me remind everyone, as I am getting the feeling that I am the only one in the entire world that remembers that the word democracy means government by the people, for the people. So that should mean the people elect the government that will work in their interest, which means there should be some form of equity, when it comes to the distribution of the countries' resources. Capitalism on the other hand, has no real definition. It depends on who you talk to and make no mistake, their response will be as sparing as the morsel they leave for the ninety percentile to scramble for. The closest capitalism gets to democracy; is government by the people for the man. And I need not say who the man is. The capitalists are so greedy that they even try to sell democracy to countries with resources so that they can have a government that they can purchase for little. But they have lost sight of the reality that 'a people's revolution' means just that, so very soon most people will eventually demand their share of their country's resources.

So where will that leave the capitalist? There is also that other capitalist myth that if there was to be an equitable distribution of every dollar to every human on the earth, it would not be long before things would end up in the same economic order as it is now. I say to these pundits, give me my share and wait for the economic wheels to stop turning and see who or what lands where.

THE VEGETARIAN
BY: LENWORTH HENRY

T-bone steak, pork chops, favorite cuts, you name it.
Rump roast, lamb hocks, chicken breast and fillet.
Eat them all; love them all, there is nothing to it.
I' m a born vegetarian; I just let the animals chew it.

(2)
I won't follow no cow to no pasture,
To chop grass and step in no mud.
The cows will come home to the barnyard,
Lay down to nibble their cuds
All day they are out there a reaping
Selecting and packing the grass,
So that this indirect vegetarian
Can stay home and sit on his ass

(3)
I was not made with incisors
Like many of them animals do
To be using my mouth as no lawn mower
Breaking teeth, slicing gum as I chew
The goats are now up in the mountain
Churning weeds in a luscious stew,
That turns up in their flesh by tomorrow
Goat head soup, what a sumptuous brew!

(4)
See that poor pig deep in the valley
No time to raise its darn head
Do you think he is having a fine time?
Chewing roots of plants long dead?
And what of the hapless chicken
Whose misfortune it happens to be
Grinding nuts that are dried from creation?
That there thing could not happen to me.

(5)
These poor guys were created as agents
To break down the raw vegetable,
Reproduce them in edible order
So that we would not have much trouble
To enjoy all of God's vegetation,
Eat, drink and be merry he said
Does it matter in what form you take it?
You still will be ending up dead.

(6)
So I won't follow no goat to no mountain
No cow to no grassy meadow
No chicken around any barnyard
No digging around like a sow
Their flesh will turn up on my table
For me to enjoy every bit
This man is a born vegetarian
I just let the animals chew it.

YES DOCTOR

The beaming beauty, bent on seduction, approached the doctor with a broad smile and said hello. The gracious young medic was impressed and thanked her for brightening up his day. When he did so, the charming chick broke into a sensual laugh, reflexively opening her mouth displaying her fairly broad lips. The doctor, in his jovially mischievous style, asked the young beauty if she knew that the size of a lady's mouth is an actual refection of some sensitive organ in her biological makeup. "Yus Ductu." was her careful, stoic reply.

MOURNING WIVES

The wife sat in the front pew with the other family members, as the funeral of her husband was in progress. The massive gathering puzzled her and she was a little confused; there could be some mistake. The time for the eulogies came and there was a lineup of some of the most eminent people waiting to make their contributions. After the first few spoke to the shouts of amen, she could take it no more. She rose and rushed to the casket and as everyone fell silent, she demanded that it be opened. Thinking that it was just a grieving wife's way of saying a special farewell to her loving husband, someone opened the casket. But instead of kissing the corpse or even giving a last touch, she loudly declared that after hearing all the great accolades directed at the deceased, she had to make sure that she was not at the wrong funeral as she never knew the man to whom everyone was showing such adoration. Convinced that it was her husband, she returned to her seat, still grumbling that she did not know that man.

NUMBER TWO

Wife number two appeared totally overcome with grief as she sat by herself and mumbled incessantly. Someone who happened by chance to get close to her, thought she had heard her repeating "Lord mi God." (Oh Lord my God). But after a while another relative leaned over from a back seat to offer a word of consolation, only to stop short when she heard what she was certain was "Lord mi glad!" (Lord I am glad). And a few other secret listeners confirmed the latter's report.

DOCTOR SEHYU DEAD

She went to the morgue to identify the body before it was placed in the storage, but it so happened that about the said time, maybe the sound of his wife's voice, helped the self-centered wife beater to miraculously rise from a coma. She lifted the sheet and the husband was so happy to see her. As soon as she saw the movement, she hurriedly covered his face and was walking away quickly when the man called out to her. Not wanting anyone to know what was happening, she went back over to him and told him to shut up as he was dead. The husband tried to get off the gurney and declared that he was alive, but the disappointed wife told him sternly that she did not care what he thought, the doctor had declared him dead, so he was dead, and with that she pushed him back and threw the cover over him and exited the hall.

Just when she thought her life would be finally free, from years of abuse, he had to come back from the dead.

BURY THE BOTTLE

She could be seen on the move just about every day, accompanied by her beloved donkey, in a little village near the border of Hanover and St James. It was a mystery how she was able to control that huge hormonal beast, when most people kept their distance on approach. But the story is not about Miss Anna and her burro; it was about how she ended up a loner, except for her faithful companion.

Yes, as the story went, she was happily married to a very well loved and industrious man, but after a while she started to suspect that her beloved spouse was developing a disease called wondering eyes. She decided not to allow it to become malignant so she went for a walk (visited an Obeah man) in Trelawney.

He gave her two bottles, one with 'Oil of Tanya' and the other with 'Oil of Tandeh.' She was firmly instructed to mix the Tanya with her husband's meals and bury the Tandeh deep in the ground.

Well, I wish I wasn't the one to tell you the outcome, after Miss Anna got the bottles mixed up. She buried her husband instead, and, im tandeh.

BIG BOY

After Brer Anancy, Big Boy was the most popular folk hero during my childhood. If you did not know a Big Boy story, you never attended school. Because they were mostly lewd and at times sexually explicit, they held a great allure and the fact that Big Boy was a menace to parson and teacher, our primary antagonists, he justly deserved hero status. Other than secretly assembling in our bush classes to learn how to work obeah to catch girls with Broom Weed and Leaf of Life, indulging in the Big Boy craze could have well been our only sin as I could never recall any of my schoolmates scoring in the obeah bid

It was school inspection day and the inspector had just finished quizzing the class about rhyming words. His next subject was Religious Education and the topic was Sampson. Big Boy especially liked that story and had his hand up before everyone else. But inspector was quizzing the whole class so Big Boy was forced to wait. Inspector asked the class what Samson did to the Philistines. After failing to get a correct response from the rest of the nervous class, Big Boy's chance came. So in the midst of him shouting 'me, inspector,' Big Boy was asked to answer the question. In his typical manner, Big Boy stood erect and loudly recited, that Samson took the jawbone of an ass, and lick the Philistines in their ('rated r'). The principal, who was observing close by, became white with embarrassment, but the inspector was very amused; it was dramatic but it rhymed and was the correct answer.

PENNARIA

St Thomas street smart guy visited downtown Kingston to do business and he was highly alert as he knew a lot about pickpockets. He was cautious about his wallet more than anything else. But the pen he displayed in his shirt pocket caught the eyes of a pair of hoodlums who knew that a Parker Pen would fetch a good price on the black market. He was turning a corner when he saw two suspicious guys eying him and each other across the narrow street. He could see that they were up to no good, so he kept his hand close to his pocket.

As soon as he passed the guy on his side of the road, he heard him say "Pennaria" to which his crony replied "Pickaria," as he started to cross the street. Quickly sensing what was about to happen, country man suddenly turned back to the nearer guy and placed a sharp ratchet knife at his throat and declared, "And I would knife out your rassaria" The two bolted in a flash.

HOLY LOAN

This young gentleman desperately wanted to go to church, but he had absolutely nothing to wear and he simply could not afford appropriate garb. Fortunately for him, a generous church going brother heard of his plight and loaned him a full outfit for the next Sunday's service. Whether by fate or design, the two ended up sitting next to each other in church that Sunday. Prayer time came and, as was the custom, everyone would kneel on the specially designed prayer cushions. The unfortunate brother was just about to do the holy honors when he was rudely admonished by his brother-lender for attempting to damage his pants by kneeling on it. Discretion was not a part of the makeup of this generous brother, and all those within earshot were embarrassed for the recipient.

At the end of the service, everyone was apologizing to this poor brother, but a particular gentleman was obviously more disturbed than the rest, so he pulled the embattled brother aside and made him an offer to furnish his clothing for the next Sunday's service, and anytime necessary. He assured him that he had absolutely nothing to worry about whenever he was wearing his clothes. And with that they parted company.

The next Sunday the whole church was full as there was a special service and there were many visitors in attendance. The sympathetic brother had delivered on his promise and this time the recipient cautiously put some space between them on the same pew. Prayer time came and as everyone was kneeling, the recipient was a bit reluctant to get to his knees and impulsively looked across to the donor, who immediately stretched across and assured him fairly loudly; "Don't be afraid to kneel man, it's my pants yu wearing, you can do anything you want with it."

WHITE WASH PIG

Everyone at the crossroad in Bailey's Vale near Port Maria shared the same story that only one hog; a white one with black belly and feet, was sold to the hog truck from Kingston. So when Mr. Singh came at full speed, from Oxford, in hot pursuit of the man whom he heard had stolen his black hog, presumably to sell to the hog truck, he was sorely disappointed and took liquor for it. He later went home a sad and puzzled man.

At about the said time that Mr. Singh's friends were showering him with liquors of sympathy, another shower was pounding the Junction main road near the St Andrew border. It was raining so heavily that the hog truck could hardly negotiate the grueling Junction road. The driver was relieved when he finally found a safe place to pull off at a gas station in Golden Spring. The rain finally subsided and the driver decided to check his cargo before hitting the road again. As he walked towards the back of the truck he noticed a white substance draining from his cab, where the pigs were. He climbed onto the rails to take an aerial view, and discovered that there was no white hog on his truck. He did a head count to see if any other hog was missing, but the mystery only thickened when he realized that according to the tally, no hog was missing. He decided to go amongst the swine and that was when he got a pleasant surprise. Standing there with all the rest of the hogs was one with a black back with white sides that were blackening faster than Mr. Singh could swallow his Puss Gin. The thief had whitewashed Mr. Singh's hog before he sold it to the truck.

The next Friday, Mr. Singh was at Bailey's Vale again, but this time to collect his black pig from the generous truck driver who had decided to cut his losses and return the black hog as he expressed hope that the pig painter would be caught

PATRONS
BY LENWORTH HENRY

If you build it they will come.
If you sell it they will buy it.
It's the object of your business,
You simply can't deny it.

But don't you wish you had the power,
To select who comes and goes,
Even if the result is,
A few dollars to lose?

They come from every culture,
Ideology and hew.
Their common goal is savings,
But quality service too.

They come with all their luggage,
But some with baggage too.
It certainly would make your day,
If none unloads on you.

But there is going to come a day,
No matter what you do,
Your loyalty will face the test,
And you may say this too.

Customers are the worst thing,
To happen to my trade.
The awful truth about it;
Without them it is dead.

ONE ARM BANDIT

The one armed man was charged with stealing a large blue seam bag of flour and had just pleaded not guilty, using his severe handicap as evidence. The judge not only appeared to have believed him, but went further to admonish the arresting officer for his callous insensitivity to that poor, almost helpless human plight. Needless to say the accused was so overwhelmed by the judge's passion that he almost started to believe he did not really steal the flour. Meanwhile, the bag of flour, which was submitted as evidence, was on the floor right in front of the judge's bench.

Continuing his scolding, the judge concluded that an injustice was done and compensation was in order. What better offer could he have made to the poor beleaguered man, but the said bag of flour, that caused his plight in the first place? He turned to the, by now, elated thief and told him to take the bag of flour and go in peace.

With unmatched dexterity, the one armed man did a twist and a turn while bending, and in no time was heading for the door with the bag of flour on his shoulder. Everyone in that courtroom was greatly amused and it was only when the judge ordered him back, did the one arm bandit see the folly of his ways

DUMB AND DEAF

Two friends used to go around town begging on a regular basis. One of them was dumb and deaf and the other was very normal, so he acted as the spokesman. After a while the spokesman became apprehensive at the fact that whenever he made his presentations, most donors handed their money directly to the handicapped man and little, if any, to him. He decided he had to find a way to profit from this venture too.

Finally, he came up with a plan to play dumb and deaf on their next outing. He was surprised at how good the scheme was working and greed made him decide to take the chance even at places they had targeted before. They were visiting the familiar Mr. Chang's grocery store, where both men were now deaf and dumb. Mr. Chang was taken aback because he had seen those two guys before and he was certain one of them actually spoke, so he, quick witted as he was, handed some money to the guy he knew to be deaf and dumb. He then turned to the still mumbling imposter and suddenly asked, "you dumb and deaf too?" "Yes sir," came the brisk reply.

THE TAIL WAS NOT PORK IAH

White squall, (hunger), was killing the Rastaman, and just when he had lost all hope of finding something to cook, what could come by, but a forbidden swine? The dread contemplated his options; face Jah hungry and pure, or partake of the accursed thing, and pine in Babylon. He did not yet decide his option, when the hog made an unexpected turn and came awfully close as he passed the desperate dread. Before he knew it, the dread had pulled out a knife and made a swipe, which missed the pig, but took its tail cleanly off.

In no time the dread had cleaned and cooked the pig's tail. He was halfway through his meal when another hungry dread, drawn by the aroma, arrived on the scene. The dread tried to hide his pot but not before the visitor looked into it.

"Dready, you eating pork Iah?" he asked in amazement. "No star." retorted the dread. "The whole hog had already passed with all of the pork, when I made the swipe, and the tail was all I got. The swine escaped with all the pork.Iah, I only got the tail."

DUMB THINGS SUFFER

The fairly wealthy country farmer was on one of his regular Friday visits to Kingston. The fishtail Chevy he was driving was competing for road space with the dozens of horse, mule or donkey drawn carts that lined the busy Ferry highway, nose to bumper, that morning. Their destination was the popular Coronation Market. There would be no surprise if an occasional accident occurred, and, as was always the case, some people were poised to capitalize on any situation that presented itself.

On that morning, this farmer had the misfortune of running into a mule drawn cart at Six Miles. The result was a mule badly wounded on the ground, groaning in agony and the driver-presumably seriously injured, lying close by and groaning even louder than the mule (He had just hit the jackpot.)

The farmer knew the law and determined that the mule was doomed, so he briskly walked over to the ill-fated animal, pulled out his licensed revolver and shot the mule point blank, thus ending its pain. He then turned, and with the same briskness, headed straight for the still groaning man, blowing the smoke from the tip of his gun as he declared; "I hate to see dumb things suffer!" If there ever was an example of a man disappearing into thin air, that was it.

SWALLOW NO DOG

After a hefty meal of rice and peas with fried chicken, a Kingstonian went to his favorite bar in Crossroads to have a drink. He ended up drinking so much that he became drunk and rushed outside to go to New York (vomit). While he was in the process, a hungry stray mongrel came by and was happy to partake of the rum laced cuisine. While still leaning against a wall for support, the stoned man momentarily opened his eyes and saw all the mess he had created and the dog there too. In his inebriated state, he did not know what to make of this scene in front of him, so he tried to figure it out loudly to himself. "I remember when I ate the rice and peas" he said "And I remember when I ate the chicken. I even remember when I drank the rum" and looking seriously puzzled he uttered, "but I swear to God I never swallow a dog."

ANYBODY SEE MISS ADA

Small farmer from Westmoreland came home one day only to find that his common law wife of many years had packed out and left the house they had shared for as long as they had been together. Heartbroken and confused, he headed for the crossroads, only to be hit with more bad news; Miss Ada,. as she was called, had actually boarded the only bus that plied the Kingston route that morning. Thinking Kingston was like his little community where everyone knew each other, he decided to board the said bus the next day to find Miss Ada. After what seemed like an eternal journey, dissecting several cities, he was finally told he had reached Kingston. He exited the bus at Coronation Market where thousands of people were moving about, and approached the first person he came upon and asked him if he saw a slim brown woman in a red frock and brown backless shoes named Miss Ada, anywhere round the place. He spent the entire day canvassing the entire downtown.

ONLY SAFE PLACE

It had become a very common occurrence for clients to be robbed by their escorts, as they slept after a night's rendezvous. Those ladies of the night would pretend to be asleep and as soon as the gentlemen fell asleep, they would raid their pockets, strip them of their jewelry or any thing of value and leave, not even collecting their pay for the night's work.

After hearing so many sad tales from his friends, this lifelong patron decided that he could never give up his favorite nocturnal pastime, so he decided that he would put an idea to the test, on his next escapade.

Round one ended, and as quickly as the lady left for the restroom, he made his move. She came out and they retired to bed. In no time she was snoring and he pretended to be out cold also. As soon as she heard his snores she shook him to test how soundly he was sleeping. After determining that he was out, she got up and went straight for his pants. As he eyed her, she rifled his pants pocket. After finding nothing, she appeared confused and for a while she just stood there. He quickly closed his eyes as she approached the bed and carefully lifted the pillow under his head. She then searched her own pillow, but found nothing. By now she was becoming desperate and she went for the mattress and raised it so hard he almost fell off, but he stayed put.

She started panting the floor, but suddenly stopped as it seemed an idea came to her; she did not search his shoes. She dived for his shoes, sure to succeed this time, but there was nothing there. She was breathing heavily when she literally fell plump! on the bed. She did not seem to care whether she woke him up or not. In one instance, she got up and picked up her bag as if to leave. At that point he got really nervous, but she quickly put it down and came back to the bed mumbling to herself. If he were really asleep her movements would surely wake him up, but he made sure not to blink an eye. For the entire night she never slept a minute and even before daylight, she shook him so hard that he could awake from the dead.

He finally got up and asked her why she had woken him up; to which she abruptly replied that she wanted her pay as she was leaving. He cautioned her to be patient and softly walked over to where her hand bag was and picked it up as she protested. She watched in absolute shock as he opened it and emptied the contents of one compartment in which he had placed all his cash and other valuables, when she went to the restroom the night before. As he handed her the dues for the night's work, she stood there frozen like a statue; her mouth wide open.

LOVE LETTER

My sweet heart throb,

I would climb the highest mountain, I would swim the deepest sea, I would cross the wildest river, just for a chance to be with thee.

(PS) If no rain tonight, you'll see me,

Forever Loyal.

DISCRETION

A very distraught woman paid a visit to her doctor, claiming to be suffering from stress as a result of her husband running off with just about everything they possessed in their matrimonial home. The caring doctor completed his diagnosis and concluded that she needed medication. After handing her the liquid medication, he instructed her to take one teaspoon full three times daily, beginning at breakfast. The woman declared that she had no teaspoon left in the house. The doctor then recommended a regular spoon and got the same response "Im gone with them too doctor." After contemplating all the options the, by now, frustrated medic made a last ditch effort to diffuse a, by then, volatile situation. "My good lady," he said "all you need to do whenever you are taking the medication is to use your discretion." "Doctor, she emphatically responded, "Him gone with all that too."

CAT-O-NINE

During the Colonial Era in Jamaica, one method of punishment frequently meted out to criminals, was the lash in and lash out, meaning, convicts were sentenced to receive whipping by means of a 'Cat-O-Nine' (a nine pronged whip), or the Tamarind Switch. The nature of the crime help determine the number of strokes a convict would receive. This particular career criminal and anti-jail advocate, was for the first time, sentenced to receive seven lashes in and seven lashes out. As a veteran of the penal system, he claimed he had received complaints of prisoners receiving more switches than the judges stipulate and he was determined to put an end to this unjust practice.

The moment for his lashing came and he was as resolute as ever, even declaring that he knew of the over whipping and it could never happen to him. He boasted that he would be setting precedence by becoming the first convict to count every stroke.

The first blow was administered to him and he powerfully and loudly barked "One!" The second one came, and all he could utter was a plaintively, ear piercing scream, "Tooooooooo." The third was a sound that rhymes with three, but it did not come from his mouth, it was 'pee' that flooded the ground. There was not another sound from then on, "Bring back the good old days".

THAT'S NOT WHAT WE CALL IT MAAM

Knighted British immigrant and well respected founder of the JSPCA in 1904, really loved Jamaica and took great pleasure in traversing every nook and cranny of her adopted paradise. She was a very overactive individual and would get to any destination by any means necessary, and by foot, was one of her favorite modes. On one of those missions to promote her project, she employed the services of a young man to be her guide. The route would take them through a very grueling and bushy short cut that led to a school she was visiting in Manchester. All along the path, she displayed a type of fitness that was incredible for her age, and which elicited a lot of praise from her guide. She would climb a wall with ease and bend low if a wire was what she had to go under. She was in a very excited mood when she realized that only one wall stood between them and their final destination.

All throughout the trip, the guide would go ahead of her and hold her hand as she negotiated wires, steep slopes or walls. But she was not too happy to appear wimpy and protested at times, and at this last wall, she decided to climb over all by herself, and all the guide could do was to stand ready in case she needed him. As he was waiting on the other side, she mounted the wall in ankle deep dress and was making her descent, when she slipped and fell on her buttocks. This resulted in her two feet spreading out widely, as her dress tail got tangled in some weeds.

The now startled guide was totally overwhelmed and embarrassed by what he had just seen, but before he knew it, the dexterous lady was back on her feet as if nothing had happened. As she did a final brush up on her skirt, she turned to the still startled guide and cheerfully asked; "Did you see my agility?" "Yes mam," he smilingly replied as he struggled not to laugh. Then after a brief pause he cautiously remarked, still smiling; "But a noh dat wi call it mam." ('that's not what we call it mam').

AMBUSHED BY A BOUNCER

Cops in a very drug-infested town in ST Catherine, decided it was time to take down a kingpin who was operating with callous indifference to law enforcement. It was also believed that he thought himself above the law as he had cops on his payroll. After months of intelligence gathering an informant provided details of the dealer's next big move to airlift marijuana from a cricket field that sometimes doubles as an illegal air strip at the back end of the little town.

The cops were told that a truck would be transporting the goods to the field on a certain day, and it would be unloaded and hidden to await the arrival of the airplane the following day. Things were certainly working in the cop's favor and they did not hesitate to plan an ambush along the narrow path that led to the small oval. As the flat bed truck covered and laden with bags from tip to tip, made its grueling ascent to the oval, the excited cops emerged from cover and made the pullover. Finally they will get their man.

As the search commenced, the cop thought nothing of the first bags just containing broom weed and coconut husk. That was just a mere decoy as the real stuff was at the bottom of the pile. They also saw nothing unusual about the heavy human traffic that headed to the oval during the operation that morning. In fact, no one had to tell them the reason why, as quite a few men were regaled in their immaculate, white cricket uniforms, gears and all. But as the search prolonged, frustration had set in. They were at it for hours and the cargo was depleting and not one ounce of marijuana was yet found.

In their exhausted state the searchers had failed to recognize that the cheers at the oval had died down, and it was not until they heard the earth-shattering sound of a twin engine jet, and saw its black and white stripes as it took to the air from the oval, did they realize they had been had, big time In their rage, they rushed to the oval, fully bent on detaining every last man woman or child on that field. But they were in for a greater surprise as the only thing that was left alive on that field was a fire that was lit as part of the plot. The cricketing crowd had simply vanished without a trace.

On follow up investigation, it was revealed that the airplane had arrived the night before but was covered at the edge of the oval. The drugs were also stored nearby and as the cricket match progressed so too was the loading process. The big man won again.

CULLUSH PUTTUSH

I attended school in this St Mary community for a short time and my friends and I took great pleasure in prying into the affairs of a family, who lived along our home route. I think I may need to adjust that statement, as we really never had to pry as every sordid detail of that couple's private life, came to us loud and profanely clear. The matriarch of that family seemed to take pride in humiliating her spouse in such a manner that we were always guaranteed entertainment on a daily basis. It seemed she must have timed her outbursts to fit into the school's dismissal schedule, as I could never imagine her being able to keep up that tirade all day. And her beleaguered and cowered companion, who had an interesting nickname, was hardly ever seen or heard from, except when we would normally add insult to injury. We would do this by choosing a down time when the abuser was not home or she was out of breath, to shout out that nickname at the gate and rush at warp speed to complete a corner before he, armed with a very sharp machete, could cut us off at a shortcut through his property. This was at a point where the property across the street was virtually inaccessible, as it was steep and well fenced. For him to beat us to that point, meant we were trapped between points and we would have a long wait until he got tired or bored. We would hope that luck came our way and a ride came along, or a more orderly group of kids came by so we could blend in and pass.

But even then, as soon as we passed, we would shout out that nickname and even poor innocent kids would be forced to run for their lives, as stones would be coming at us from seemingly every angle. Fortunately for everyone, except for many falls in the sprints, no one was ever injured or chopped up. And just when we thought that things at that home could not have gotten more dramatic, it did.

I arrived at school one Monday morning, only to hear whispers that there was a big development at our place of entertainment and the tormented had actually gotten a new name. 'Cullush Puttush.' As the tale goes, the matriarch was ill over one weekend and was unable to accompany her spouse to the Coronation Market in Kingston, where they usually take their food products for sale. That was the first time he was going alone and it turned out to be a total disaster

As I heard it, everything went smoothly up to his laying out of the goods in the normal way in the market. But he had a certain weakness, which was well known to many of the female vendors, who sat near their stall. He was a peeping tom. He would not pass up an opportunity, even in front of his wife, to steal a peek at any unsuspecting female across from him. Some of them were annoyed by this, but chose not to inform his wife for fear of being bomb blasted by her. She had a reputation in that place. So, on seeing him all by himself, the vendors crafted a plot to give him his fill of views and in the process rob him blind. As one set of women sat provocatively across from him, he immediately became distracted and the ones beside and behind him almost emptied his stall, leaving him with just enough to pay for his transportation home.

On his return home, he had told his wife that he was beaten and robbed and he may have faked some bruises and she was skeptical, but waited for the next weekend to investigate.

She arrived at the market that Saturday, only to learn that her mate's robbery was the talk of the town. No details were denied her. She was told in graphic details how he reacted to the exposures and at one point, he was so absorbed that he shouted 'Cullush Puttush!' That did it for her and he paid the price. One afternoon she was overheard admonishing him for choosing cullush abroad, over cullish at home, whatever that meant. Needless to say, with an added nickname, our trips home became more action packed.

THE GATES OF HELL

He was a hardworking man and a pillow in his small community in Westmoreland. He also owned and operated a bar in the community. But for reasons he himself could not understand, his bar started experiencing decline in sales and he became concerned that someone had cast an obeah spell on him and he started complaining a lot. This got the attention of a nearby obeah man's scout, who was always looking out for vulnerable people to scam. He was at the bar one afternoon and listened as the bar owner literally spilled his soul to some patrons. He made a note of what he heard. When he left the bar, he headed straight to his boss who was more than delighted at the prospect of a new client.

The very next day the obeah man went on a mission, which took him to that targeted bar. His partner-in-crime happened to be there from earlier on. There were quite a few patrons at the bar when the obeah man arrived. No sooner had he entered, he started looking around, as if he was staring into space. Everyone was curious but kept their silence. He took a seat and ordered a flask of White rum. As soon as he was served he poured some into a glass and proceeded to take a sip. The liquid did not quite reach his mouth when he rose suddenly and threw the contents of the glass against the nearby wall. He then picked up the flask, did a three sixty turn, and uttered something loud, but incoherent as he simultaneously flashed the bottle in front and above him, emptying the contents all over the bar, even dosing some of the stunned patrons. He then left the bar in a hurry, as he continued mumbling to himself.

All those present were dumbstruck; they had never seen anything like that before. Something seemed to be wrong in that bar and they began to wonder. The bar owner was beside himself with shock. A total stranger seemed to have given some credence to his demonic claims and he reiterated his belief to his patrons who now appeared less skeptical, even supportive. He was asking himself who was that man, when the scout declared that he had seen him somewhere, but could not recall where. Everyone seemed curious to know who that strange visitor was and was glad when the scout promised to investigate. He came back a few days later with the good news that he discovered the identity of the stranger and he was told that he was fairly new to the area and operated a balm yard about four miles away on the border with St Elizabeth. He even had more details about the operation, which include the time of night a new client should visit; and that was midnight. The bar owner was very happy for the information and even told the informant that he would certainly visit the next day. He even served him quite a few free drinks.

The next night, close to midnight, the barman chartered a friend's car and was dropped off close to the balm yard, from where he had to complete the last half mile alone. His friend knew where he was going and reluctantly drove off, leaving him behind. He had strong reservations about leaving him, but he never questioned when he was told to leave, as he thought his passenger would have been staying overnight.

Nervously, the visitor approached the spooky and poorly lit house and softly tapped on the door. A woman in a white gown and colorful head wrap greeted him and ushered him in. He entered this hall that had something like a shrine in the middle. He was offered a seat in, what appeared like, a shed, covered with zinc and coconut limbs for wall. He was still nervously looking around when he heard a male voice call out his name and other personal details of his life, no stranger could know. He continued in this diatribe, condemning the evil culprit who was responsible for the man's pain and suffering. All this was going on inside an adjacent solid building, and the speaker had not even dared to come outside to see what his visitor looked like. How could he have known who he was without asking him? And how could he have gotten such details about his life? He never had to wait long, as the ghostly figure with a painted face atop a long black gown, emerged and declared that his crystal ball told no lies. His visitor's whole life was clear as daylight and fortunately for him, he had come to the right place and not a day too soon. The barman was now on full surrender and appeared like a lamb to the slaughter. If he could read him that well, he could put his whole life in his hands

The healer spared no time in outlining his plan and even when he revealed his fee, the lifelong tight wad made no objection. He was here to be free of a spell and that was all that mattered. The ritual went through smoothly, except for some serious struggles the healer claimed he had with the notorious, coolie duppy. But that was taken care of. But he had some very serious warning for the barman. Everything was in place for the wicked spell to break, but its total success rest with the barman, who would have to play a vital role on his way home. From previous experience dealing with obeah men, the barman knew that the healers always insist that they walk home after the ritual and also cannot allow day to light out on them before they reach home. So he had planned to use a shortcut that would not only reduce his journey by nearly a mile, but he would avoid a church cemetery that everyone claimed was haunted. But that plan would not be working that night, as he was sternly warned not to use the shortcut, as the ghosts he had just expelled could make a last ditch effort to follow him home and break the spell. If he used the long road by the church, no strange ghosts could pass there so he could never be followed home. He went on to emphasize that if the spell is broken, it could result in the demise of both parties, especially him, the healer. Barman must walk all the way, no running. And on his way, he should not react to any sound, even if he heard sounds like the gates of hell were opened and all hell broke loose, he should never run, as that would mess up the plan and endanger lives.

He finally dismissed the barman after reiterating his warning, and that shivering soul quietly descended the incline, fearing the very sound of his heart beat. But as he made his way home, he was certain he was being followed by the unfriendly ghosts and made regular glances backwards to make sure they were not close. On many occasions he wanted to run at the simplest sound, but he knew his life and future depended on him walking all the way. All along though, he could never see how he could muster enough courage to approach that pitch dark curve that announced his approach to that haunted church cemetery. Even when he had company, they always run when they were negotiating that spot. But now he was alone, how was he going to do it?

He was now on tip toes as he approached a very tall mango tree that literally formed an arch over the road at the entrance to the church gate, where most of the graves stood. He had reached the epicenter of his fears and was just making his breathless way pass it, when the gates of hell opened and all hell broke loose, and it came from the mango tree above his head.

In a matter of minutes he collapsed at his front door and his wife who heard the commotion, came out and assisted him inside. Never before could he have done that mile and a half in a full sprint, and as he was coming to, the ominous reality of his pending demise hit home. He knew he had to visit the obeah man as soon as he could, so at first light, he headed back to the balm yard. As he approached, an angry and seemingly out of control male voice, shouted at him to leave his property never to return, as he had almost cost him his life. He had blown the one chance to help save himself, and he could never help him again. He recommended another obeah man that he could see, and he left.

The bewildered barman was left with no other choice but to turn and wobble down the hill with his hands on his head. No mention was made of a refund. But if he had looked towards the altar in the thatch shed, he would have seen the drums and the tambourine that the scout had just brought back from the church gate, and a closer look would reveal a sleeping soul, worn out from that all night vigil.

As the barman descended the hill, fearful and dejected, he could not help but marvel at the omniscience of his exploiter. Just how did he seem to know everything, including the fact that he actually ran that morning?

SET UP GOAT

The Trelawney police were alerted to look out for a vehicle transporting goats stolen from a certain community, very late one night. As a result, roadblocks were set up at strategic points leading from the area. At one of those checkpoints, a pickup truck was pulled over. It was one with a covered cab and rails all around. One officer peered through the narrow openings and observed some sort of movement. Suspicious, he retrieved a flashlight and proceeded to do a more thorough inspection. What he saw was a lot of felt hats lined up as if on the heads of people sitting on benches arranged in the cab for passengers. But something else stirred his curiosity; the heads wearing those hats were all in a perpetual nod; up and down. The truck driver was asked to explain the strange behavior of his passengers, at which time he informed the cops that they were on their way from a setup (a wake) and his passengers were all drunk, hence the constant nodding. It seemed plausible enough so the driver was sent on his way.

It was not long after, that a colleague from another jurisdiction arrived on the scene with what seemed to be a vivid description of the suspected getaway vehicle. It accurately matched the pickup that was checked out and released earlier. A call ahead led to an interception of the vehicle which turned out to contain live cargo, but not drunken wake goers, but goats; stolen goats, all crowned in felt hats for disguise. Now you know what all that nodding was about.

CAYMANAS PARK

Caymanas Park is the proverbial den of iniquity. This moment a sinner prays and the next a Christian cusses. From the three card man, with his confederates, who would be trying to rip off some naive country man or woman, to the tipster who collects winnings in every race, as he is always able somehow, to promote every horse in each race as a sure winner to his gullible circle of pundits.

MINI HA HA

You could see the trucks in Saint Mary, transporting bananas and market people and the occasional groups on tours. 'Mini Ha Ha,' was boldly emblazoned all over them. As I heard it, the trucks were named after a horse with the same name. Mini Ha Ha was a thorough bred filly that dominated sprint racing during her heyday at the Caymanas race tracks. She ranked with the likes of Bunny Blue Flag and Kandahar, which were legendary in their day. As the story goes, this St Mary man owned one or two trucks and he wasn't doing badly at all. He had managed to save up enough to purchase new trucks and so he planned a trip to Kingston to check the dealerships out. He was not alone and he had no reason to protest when his traveling companions, who were compulsive gamblers, suggested a detour via Caymanas Park Racetrack. What was promised to be a brief stop, just to see a tipster, ended up as an extended visit.

As is normal at the tracks, one can easily get caught up in the euphoria. Mini Ha Ha was a favorite in an upcoming race and from all indications, she was sure to win that race. As a favorite, she would not pay a lot to win, so to make money from her win, one had to buy big. After a few entreaties from one career gambler, the trucker decided to put down a huge bid on this sure shot.

Then came the announcement from the loudspeaker; "And now the gates are open and the horses jump, and Mini Ha Ha takes the lead. She is moving away from the field and seems to have this race all by herself." As the lead was extending, so was the momentum of the crowd and to an even greater degree, that group from St Mary.

The elated trucker, who was reluctant at first, was now the loudest in the group. As the horses approached the turn for home Mini Ha Ha's lead began to shorten and another horse was gaining on the outside. The trucker was still shouting 'Mini Ha Ha, Mini Ha Ha,' but his voice was fading with the horse's prospect. As they approached the winning pole Mini Ha Ha was overtaken, and at that time, all that was uttered by the broken trucker was, 'Mi-niiiii, Haaa Ha!' And with that he collapsed and kicked the bucket. Incredibly, Mini Ha Ha found some reserved energy and actually came back and won by a neck, but the ill-fated trucker only learnt that in the here after, and his wife not only honored his wishes from the windfall, but she appropriately named the fleet of trucks.

NINE MONTHS

Mass Charlie met this young lady and was showing her off to everyone. Within a couple of months, and to everyone's surprise, she was displaying signs of pregnancy and Mass Charley was ecstatic about his prowess. He was on top of the world. However, the puzzled country folk, including family members, were not amused and they made no bones about expressing it to Mass Charley, who only dismissed them as being envious. Within about four months of being with Mass Charley, the damsel gave birth to a bouncing full term baby boy, who bore, not the least resemblance to mass Charley, let alone his complexion and race. But the proud new mom promptly named the baby after Mass Charley.

Needless to say, the rumors escalated and Mass Charley was getting overwhelmed with ridicule. Finally, he mustered enough courage to confront the young lady about the rumors. He reiterated the fact that it takes about nine months for a child to be born and they had not been together for near that long. But before Mass Charley could say much more, the damsel lashed back. "How long me deh wid you?" (How long have I been with you?) She asked. "Just four and a half months" replied Mass Charley. "And how long you deh wid mi?" (How long have you been with me?) "Four and a half months," Mass Charley again answered. "Then when you add four and a half to four and a half, how much do you get?" She angrily asked, "Nine months" Mass Charley responded. "You are right you know," a defeated Mass Charlie conceded, "I did not look at it that way." That did it, Mass Charley was hooked.

BE QUIET GOAT

The latest addition to the farm was a pair of noisy nanny goats. Just to hear them greet each other was annoying enough for Mrs. Pig. But when they were in the mating exercise, things really got disgusting and she shared her concern with her mate, who was freer to roam the surrounding, as she had to stay near her young brood. She even had reservation about losing her status as the most productive member of the farm, to that shameless she goat.

Not very long after, the mate woke her up one early morning with the great news that the ewe had just delivered two frisky kids. She was expecting to hear that she was still in the process of delivery, as she would be. But when she was told that that was it, she could hardly restrain herself. "All that noise for just two? And we got twelve with just a mere grunt." Mrs. Pig uttered.

DENTURES FOR A NAG

A St James farmer went to St Elizabeth to purchases horses. He did a detailed inspection of the horses before he purchased them, but he was especially impressed with one particular horse that had very sound and beautiful teeth. (A confirmation of youth) So he paid handsomely for him. Back at his farm the next day, he put the new horses out to graze. He was particularly excited about that special purchase and had his friends and neighbors over to see his good fortune. They noticed however, that the specially prized purchase seemed to be having difficulty chewing like the rest of the horses, so they did an inspection of its mouth. Lo and behold, they discovered that the beautiful array of teeth was nothing but a full mouth of dentures. That was nothing to grin about.

GRAZING IN SHADES

Prolonged droughts in some parishes like Clarendon and Saint Elizabeth, wreak havoc for livestock farmers, and only ingenuity can help them survive. One Saint Ann farmer told me that on one of his annual trips to Clarendon to purchase drought ridden cattle from a farm, he noticed that cows in a dried up pasture were gingerly grazing with some strange contraptions on their faces. He thought it strange that the cows were grazing on the dried grass as he knew that his cows in Saint Ann would never eat that grass. His curiosity led him to deduce that the cows were actually fitted with what looked like sunglasses and on enquiry that was confirmed by the farmer. He wanted an explanation for this strange practice and was told that the shades were all green. He went on to explain that the cows would never eat the grass if they knew it was dry so with the shades, they only saw green.

Please don't try that in St Ann, or St Mary, as you would never hear the end of it.

WHO LICK JOHN?

The duo was a menace wherever they went, but when it came to dances, they were crashers and wreckers. One was a puny, five footer named John and the other by contrast, a towering and super imposing six footer plus, weighing hundreds. They would attend dances just to make trouble and John was the linchpin. He would pick a fight with anyone, as he knew his Goliath of a mate would come to his aid and wreak havoc in the dance hall. Their fame had spread far and wide and no one wanted to have them as guests at their party or dance. No one any where, let alone, the friendly citizens of Buff Bay in Portland. But it was there, of all the places that the duo chose as their next port of call.

It was well into the Easter Monday dance and the crowd was rocking, when the pair made their entry. John as usual, headed for the bar and ordered drinks. His mate followed but did not sit near him. After a few drinks John decided he wanted to dance and headed into the crowd. Whatever may have transpired in that dimly lit dance hall that night left John screaming and running for his life. His sidekick heard the screams and recognized that it came from John. Something big must have gone down, as he had never heard his set-on scream that way before and he moved into action.

As he rose, John rushed up to him, and pointed to the direction where he was attacked. Without hesitation, he headed towards the dance crowd. But John did not lead him to his attacker as he usually would, instead, he lingered behind. The crowd suddenly realized who was in their midst, when the towering creature, with the thunderous voice asked; "Who lick John?" As he lumbered forward, the crowd sheared on his approach. The music also went dead and people were scrambling for cover everywhere, some jumping through windows. The super crasher was getting angrier and angrier as he continued to hear John's screams. As he approached what was left of the massive gathering, he kept on asking "Who lick John?" He had just thrown the last fleeing reveler out of the way, when something or someone rose in front of him and blocked his path. As he gazed in shock, the image rose to full height, thumped his chest and declared loudly "Mee lick John!" Not knowing what to do in his frozen state, all the notorious dance crasher could utter in a very subdued voice was "John got a big lick to-(rated, r)!" And with that he turned and beat a hasty exit from the building, the still screaming John in toe. The guys in Buff Bay knew they were coming and were prepared. That heavyweight boxer was a native.

A WHO PUSH MI?

In a small community near the Martha Brae River in Trelawney, a brazen alligator was creating havoc, by attacking livestock and terrorizing the scared coastal dwellers. Finally, after one more resident came face to face with the reptile in her yard one night, the community decided it had had enough, so by the hook or the crook, something had to be done to rid the community of this menace. The community met the following day and decided to trap the creature one way or the other. But luck seemed to be on their side, for no sooner than sunrise the following morning, everyone was awakened by loud shouts coming from a farmer who had a small well on his property. He had gone to fetch water, as he does every morning for his livestock, and came upon this angry reptile trapped in the well after its efforts to climb the steep, slippery edges had failed. As the crowd encircled the small pool, a type of circus atmosphere developed and people were having fun as they contemplated how to capture the angry predator. Killing it outright was not an option as the creature was protected by law, and the news had reached the local media.

A number of individuals had carried ropes but their effort to lasso the creature proved more and more futile as the water got more and more murky and the reptile more elusive. Everyone was becoming restless when someone joked that they needed a volunteer who could jump into the pool and wrestle the creature into submission like that crazy Australian guy on TV. The laughter did not quite subside when everyone heard what appeared to be a splash and realized that someone seemed to have taken up the challenge.

The crowd held their breath as they watched one of their own resurface, only to face the oncoming beast. Suddenly, it appeared their imperiled neighbor underwent a transformation, for no sooner had the reptile approach him with its mouth opened, he lunged at it and a fierce struggle ensued. The display of agility and dexterity by this farmer was astounding, but no one could guess what the outcome would be. In the melee someone threw a rope, which the wrestler somehow manage to use to entangle the now exhausted reptile, and with another rope, he was able to secure its mouth, and in no time the reptile was pulled from the small well.

The hero of the day could hardly leave the pool before he was mobbed by the jubilant crowd. Someone had to pull him away to safety before he was injured. For quite a while the muddy and extremely exhausted daredevil did not utter a word. The local media representatives had by then rushed to do an interview with the man of the moment. Everyone was relieved when it appeared he was ready to talk. A lot of praises were being heaped on the hero but he did not seem too amused, instead he even shrugged off some of the comments and even appeared angry.

Finally, he told the reporters that he was willing to speak and all cameras and recorders were focused. He began by saying that he was glad that he was the one who captured the reptile and he acknowledged the ovations from everyone present, but he had one very important question to ask, and it was. 'Who the ('r rated c'), pushed mi inna di well?'

OVERWEIGHT MY CAR

I offered a lady a ride in my car. She was carrying a well laden basket on her head and was grateful for the offer. When I opened the door to let her in, I noticed she never tried to take the basket from her head. She had even tried to enter the car with the basket still on her head. I must confess that I feel apprehensive about sharing the humor in this little encounter, because I was humbled by the gracious lady's humility and I know she was by no means stupid. Curious, I asked her why she would want to keep the basket on her head in the car. Her reply was simply that she did not want to put anymore weight than I already had in the car, so she just wanted to keep the load on her head to prevent that.

PEPPER IN THE POT

A young, happy family in Browns Town owned a poodle which was the pride and joy of everyone. They named him Pepper as he was very territorial and feisty. One day the lady of the house had an appointment to see the doctor so she asked her niece to come and baby sit her kids. She had put a big pot of water with red peas on the fire but in her haste had forgotten to put the meat in it to slowly cook for the soup she would prepare on her return. As she hastily departed the yard, she called out to her niece to put pepper in the pot when the water started boiling. She said nothing about meat.

When the water started boiling the niece put pepper in the pot. On her return the aunt detected a strange aroma coming from the kitchen and it did not seem to contain the spicy flavor. She had also noticed that her heart throb did not greet her at the door. But the food was more important as her husband would soon be returning from work famished. As she rushed to change her clothes she asked her niece if she had put pepper in the pot, to which she replied yes. But still not convinced, she asked her if she had put it in long enough for it to cook, as she did not smell it. "Mi put pepper inna di pot so long auntie, im bwile till him teet kin!" Came the horrific response.

Well, the niece held no grudge for Pepper, even though he had bitten her once before, but there was no meat in the pot.

MORE SILLY GIRLS

It happened back in the days when the railroad from Ewarton, St Catherine, was the means by which cattle and other livestock were shipped from St Mary and St Ann to Kingston and other parts of Jamaica. How did that happen? Well, as I was told Walkerswood and Moneague were communities through which hundreds of livestock were driven every week to the holding pens in Ewarton, to await shipment. If I am not mistaken, that may have been how Walkerswood got its name. I know it was once a through road linking St Ann to St Catherine, Kingston, and other central parishes. And although there were horses, donkeys and mules, people, I was told, mainly walked. Imagine herding wayward restless cattle across the crooked steep and rugged path through Walkerswood and Moneague and Mount Diablo? And I was also told that most of the herding took place at nights as the cattle could die from exhaustion in the daylight sun. No wonder there were so many ghost stories related to that era. But Moneague was the layover where herders would rest and recharge at the many shops in the sleepless town before continuing their journey, and it was usually after those stopovers in the bars that herders would recite stories of seeing and hearing dead herders still on the trail, as if they were still alive.

But the reason I have written this piece is just to report an incident that occurred at a little food shop in this little town during the herding days.

A group of herders had stopped at this little shop to get a snack. They were very hungry and everything in the glass case looked tempting. But the grater cakes looked the most alluring and everyone ordered one, and the two teenage sisters were thrilled to see how well business was going. The men were well into their cake when one skeptic remarked that the cakes tasted so good, he wondered if they were clean. The older of the girls wasted no time, as she gleefully replied, "Them very clean Sah, fah mamma mek wi wash wi mouth clean, clean, even with chew stick, before wi chew the coconut Sar." Well you can guess the rest.

ANOTHER SILLY GIRL

Although she lived close to the river, she could not venture there or anywhere else without her parents' permission. And her mother was the worse of the two, when it came to punishment, so when some friends came at her gate and inveigle her to accompany them for a swim, she asked them if they thought she was crazy. They were surprised at her response and questioned her reason. She stared them straight in the faces, and with her hands akimbo, firmly declared that if she went to that river and drown, her mother would kill her.

DIGNITY PERSONIFIED

He was the principal during the first year of my tenure at College in Kingston. His alias was The Keps. He was as close to infallible as any human could get. One rumored example of his propriety was that he even prayed before indulging in the procreative exercise with his wife. I am starting to sound like him now. Before the prayer is offered, both parties were usually formally attired, he, in his trade mark dark suit and tie and she preferably in a gown. I graciously solicit the approval of my, Most Noble Cows, to publish this famous prayer of the great one. "Oh God, it is not for the sweetness of it, but as you have ordained, that we should be fruitful, multiply and replenish the earth" (auth). And after every stroke, both parties would repeat the refrain 'We beseech thee to hear us, O God.'

There were some of my colleagues, who had been skeptical about the purity of this great character, but they were in for a rude awakening one morning at general assembly at the Great Quadrangle.

The Keps was making the typical announcements after worship, and as he touched on the long overdue subject of the proposed increase in lunch allowance, everyone was all ears and you could hear a pin drop when he introduced the topic. In his typical, most gracious form, he announced, "I am pleased to inform everyone present that as of next Monday the lunch allowance will be increased by a thirty three and a third percent increment on thirty cents." He had to go around that entire circle to avoid using the word forty. Why?

Some keen listener had the answer, for as quickly as the cheering died down, a voice from behind the big tree at the rear of the assembly screamed out; "Kiss mi neck! Keps could not say forty cents because there is 'fart' in it."

Even the entire faculty seated on the platform next to The Keps, could not restrain themselves from the explosion of laughter that followed that scream.

TOO DARK TO HEAR

I had negotiated a placement for one of my students in a coveted 4-H vocational training programs and he had to be at an interview early the next morning. There was no other means to inform him but to visit his home. I had had a very hectic day and could not reach the home until well into the night. After getting some directions, I finally drove up to the gate, which was very close to the road and blew the horn. It was obvious that they had all gone to bed, but I knew they were half expecting me and with good news, they would not mind the disruption. The kids heard the news I came to give and were even celebrating, when grandma, not to be outdone, shouted out "Turn on the light, the place is so dark, I can't even hear what the gentleman is saying."

FUNERAL IN ROCK

A family that is very close to mine lost a patriarch and I attended the funeral on a beautiful Sunday afternoon in a hilly little community near Mocho in Clarendon. What was slated to be a solemn occasion turned out to be anything but. From the outset some mentally challenged young family member had decided to kick a dent into every car that was parked on the scene. I actually was part of the restraining team that wrestled him to the ground. He was taken away by some family members who obviously were upset with our action, although no one seemed to want to take responsibility for the damage that was already done to some cars.

After breathing a sigh of relief that my car was spared, I eventually mounted the steep incline to the church, just in time to hear what sounded like an uproar and saw people rushing up and down. The hearse had arrived and the viewing was in progress, when whispers started going around that the body was not that of the deceased. The whispers became shouts and the shouts became screams and pandemonium broke out everywhere. In the melee, sharp divisions developed between family members, who by then seemed poised for a riot.

A call was made to the funeral home in May Pen and they were told that there was no mistake made. That still did not satisfy the skeptics. Associates and friends of the family joined in and finally an elderly man, who was said to be a close friend of the deceased, shouted for calm. He suddenly assumed the role of mediator and questioned why some mourners did not think the body was that of the deceased, to which someone replied that the corpse was too dark and the brother had lighter skin. Someone mentioned that that was not enough, as bodies get darker when people die. Another person asked about special marks and that was when things got bizarre and the drama peaked. A lady who stood just in front of me, shouted that she can prove it, as the deceased had one missing tooth in the back of his right upper jaw. "Just who could that lady have been? She was not the wife." The restless crowd sighed with relief; Finally matters would be resolved.

The mediator asked someone to open the, by then, closed coffin and at least half a dozen volunteers rushed to the scene as if in a haste to get it all over with. Most of the gathering including me, trailed behind. In no time the coffin was opened and volunteers were hovering over the head of the deceased with its sealed mouth. At that moment I suddenly cringed at the thought of witnessing such grossly disgusting exercise. But I was not alone; the volunteers' brakes jammed too, as they suddenly realized that to get to the proof, someone had to bell the cat. But that was no live cat; it was opening the mouth of a man that had been dead for days. I have to tell you that at that point, I had to beat a hasty retreat, as my reaction could be viewed as disrespectful to the deceased. And maybe not; as, come hell or high water, he had to have gotten a good laugh too or he would be dead serious.

I never really attended the ceremony as; again, I was recruited to transport one of the skeptics to the funeral home, as she wanted to make sure that none of the bodies left there was her dad's. By the time we returned everything was all over. Proof or not the old man was laid to rest. When the skeptic alighted from my car and was told that, she let off a scream that had everyone, once again, rushing to the scene. She was a professional crier and she had missed out on the chance, of a lifetime, to perform at her very dad's funeral.

THE UNRIGHTEOUS DREAD

A fairly wealthy Rasta man from Hopewell in Hanover went to Kingston with a lot of cash to do some big shopping and return home the same day. Unfortunately for him, the bus took forever to reach the city so it was late for him to do his shopping. He decided to overnight in the city. Being a tight wad, that dread had no intentions of using any of his hard earned money on lodging in Babylon. He pledged to sleep under the stars and Jah would take care of him. After a long search, he saw a parked truck that he decided was going nowhere and he settled under it for the night. He was fast asleep when some town dread happened upon him. They thought they should know all the dreads in the area, but they did not recognize that one. Where did he come from?, they wondered, and why was he sleeping under a truck and exposing himself to such danger? What sort of dread would do that?

They decided to check him out. They shook him, but he did not wake up. The long trip had taken its toll and the poor dread was out like a light. The town dreads decided to search him. Imagine their shock when they discovered the wad of cash. Righteous as they professed to be, they could not resist the temptation to rob him, and that's exactly what they did. They decided to leave him, but they were having misgivings that they had just robbed one of their own and Jah may not be pleased. But they easily found a rationale that they were certain Jah would understand; that dread was much too careless to be a righteous dread, and to make their case more strong, they decided to shave the sleeping country dread's locks. The well rested dread woke up the next morning and felt some strangeness. The first thing he did was to check for his money. When he found none, he was confused and said. "Don't tell me they rob I!" Then he sensed the unusual coldness and emptiness on his head and felt it with his hands. Realizing that there were no locks, he said with relief "No, It's not I."

NOW I KNOW DAD

Highly respected politician was asked by his young son to explain the system of government and he broke it down very practically to him. He told him that he, as the head of the household, represented the government. His mom was the manager. He, the son was the country and their helper was the working class. The son seemed to have grasped the concept right away and went on his curiously merry way.

He may have been too merry that day as he ate too many ripe bananas and suffered a bad case of diarrhea the following night. In his messy state, he rushed to his mother's room only to find her sound asleep and his attempts to arouse her proved futile. He rushed to the helper's quarters, only to stop short when he heard compromising sounds, one, the voice of his dad, coming from the room. He had no other choice but to rush back to his room messy and confused.

He hardly slept that night as he tried to put things into perspective. Still drowsy and contemplative, he went to his dad as soon as he woke up and wasted no time to let him know that he finally understood what he had been explaining about the work of government. When he was asked to elaborate, he recited the experience of the previous night. He emphasized that while the country was in a horrible mess, the management was fast asleep, as the government 'abused' the working class. (N.B), a bolt could perform the same exercise.

TELL NO MAN

As a child growing up in bush country, I always feared coming into contact with any man with long unkempt hair. I usually thought they were jail escapees, who were on the run and hiding in the woodlands, and had no means of cutting or shaping their hair. And the governments of the time did their bit by maligning the Rastafarians because of their use of marijuana. In many quarters in Jamaica, the Rastaman was feared and they knew it, but instead of giving in to the pressure and renounce their religion, they got stronger and see themselves as the oppressed in Babylon. The wisdom of the true Rastaman was well known throughout the island and other religious zealots would be best advised not to take on a Rastaman in a religious free for all. Whereas a Christian sees himself as a follower of Christ, a Rastaman sees himself as a God-man. How could you argue with that man?

This lady was walking on a narrow street in Kingston and as she turned a corner, she almost collided head on, with a Dread who was coming out of an alley. She was so frightened that she shouted "Jesus Christ!" On hearing that, the Rastaman put one finger closely to his lips and whispered to the trembling woman "Tell no man that thou seest me!" and with that, he vanished even before the startled woman could regain her composure.

FOREIGN TRAVEL

When I was a kid, it was almost everyone's dream to have a relative abroad and even more exciting, to have that individual go on farm work in Canada or the U.S. Who could forget the Denim Jeans and the big boots, the gold ring on every finger, the gold tip on every tooth and the cow chains dragging the necks down? And if that was not enough, the American slang. But that was not exclusively the farm workers' habit, just about anyone who had visited a foreign country, no matter how long, made sure the slang was the signature evidence.

I heard of this girl from Round Hill, who went to Canada for two months, leaving her loving pet pig behind. Before she left, the normal way to chase away a pig was 'choo' She returned however, totally twanged out, even forgetting her loyal pet, who by then, had grown much larger and heavier. The hog heard her voice but it was now tethered to a tree because of its size. He was so happy to hear his old companion's voice, that he struggled and got his foot out of the rope. As was usual for him, the happy hog went upon his hind legs with his front feet upon his old mistress. She tried to chase him off, as she could hardly stand her ground because of the weight. But instead of saying, 'choo!' all she was saying was "Stuer! Stuer!" But the excited hog did not relent and she fell to the ground with the pig on top of her, biting and digging at her in play. And that was when she shouted "Chooooooo!" And the pig got off her.

VISA WOES

Two lifelong friends, with almost identical socio-economic dispositions, decided that they both would like to explore the prospect of acquiring visitors' visas for the United States. The first friend visited the embassy and was asked many questions by the official. Some of the enquiries were; if he was married, if he had a permanent job, if he owned a home, and if he had savings in the bank, and so on. To each question, his answer was yes. The last question came, and it was, if he owned a car, to which he responded, no. Immediately the officer informed him that he was unable to grant him a visa at such time. On his way home, he scolded himself for not answering yes, to the car question as he was sure that if he did, he would have procured a visa.

Back home, his friend and colleague could hardly wait to hear of the outcome of the embassy visit. The visitor spared no details about his ordeal and both of them shared the conclusion that the car question was the spoiler. Friend number two felt really sorry for his colleague but was grateful that he had learned never to make the same mistake on his visit, which was the following day.

The next day he was up early armed with all the documents he considered appropriate. He took a cab as he never owned a car, but when he got to the embassy he would surely own one, the one which would drive him in style home with his glistening visa. The questions came in almost the same order as they did with his friend the day before and the yes responses slid off his lips like oil. Then the question about the car was asked and his delight reached fever pitch; that was the magic moment. Confidently and smoothly he answered yes, and the response hit him like a Mike

Tyson punch. "I am sorry sir, but I am unable to furnish a visa for you today, however, you can try again in the near future."

What both of them later discovered, was that they were both unfortunate to be interviewed by the same officer, who was just filling in for a colleague for the two weeks they were interviewed, and he did not care much about giving visas. The following week both their wives and children got visas, car or no car.

MOVE THAT THING

This goodly gentleman was at an upscale bar and lounge, in New Kingston. He was drinking and smoking, when a waiter pushed a spittoon close enough for his use. Not knowing what it was he angrily protested and demanded its removal. The waiter informed him that he was instructed to place it there. The, by now, angry socialite threatened that if it were not removed immediately, he would be spitting in it. When the waiter did not respond, that's exactly what the patron did, he spat in it.

SPECIES OF BUTTERFLY

This farm worker from Saint Catherine had just arrived at, the then, Palisados Airport in Kingston, and although there were much cheaper modes of transport to his home, he decided to charter a cab to arrive in style. On the way from the airport, the poor cab driver could hardly understand a word spoken by this man, who had actually attended the same school he attended. He was sitting in the back and a wasp suddenly flew into the car and lodged on the rear window. The foreigner's attention was suddenly turned to the wasp that kept on moving. He was expressing such great admiration for the beautiful creature, and proceeded to follow its trail with his fingers, even touching it momentarily. As they approached Ferry Highway, the curious passenger asked the driver; "What species of butterfly is this?" The stunned driver was now beside himself with annoyance and wished for a miracle. And it came not much longer, for as the foreigner was still playing with the, by then, agitated wasp, it lashed out, delivering a vicious sting on the nose of its tormentor, who now screamed at the top of his voice; "Wasp, you (b, rated, c)!"

SCAMMER EXTRAORDINAIRE

He was a regular on the farm work circuit to Florida, but his dream of getting rich by honest means, was not panning out, so he decided to achieve it by any means necessary. After his last attempt at a major injury on a farm in Florida failed, he felt time was running out on him, so he made a last ditch effort, by faking a fall from the steps as he was deplaning at the Palisados Airport in Kingston. On examination, the doctors failed to find any injury that could warrant major treatment, let alone compensation. Still he constantly complained of severe pains and the doctors tried many ways to ease his dilemma. Finally, after many referrals, the doctors decided on an operation, which only ended up with him making a new claim that he had become partially impotent. That triggered a new lawsuit, with his wife claiming that she had lost the sexual pleasures with her husband of many years. I think that case is still languishing in the courts as he had gotten no where with it.

Fast forward to the seventies, and he was a passenger on a country bus that plied the Kingston to Highgate route via Riversdale. The bus was on the return trip near Riversdale when it ran off the road and fell down a precipice and into the river below. There were quite a few injuries, but remarkably, Mr. Opportunist sustained none. Maybe because it was his first real accident, he was not prepared to capitalize, or he was so caught up in the moment that he did not realize that he had become the chief rescuer. He was transporting the injured up the very steep incline single-handedly, to the road above, from where they were being transported to the Linstead Hospital.

He had just taken the last victim to the road, when one of his life long friends, who came to view the wreck, approached him and whispered something in his ears. Immediately he collapse to the ground and passed out and no one could revive him. He was rushed to the hospital even before some of the serious victims, as his case had appeared direr.

As it was in the beginning, so it was again; déjà-Vu After a battery of tests, no symptoms were diagnosed. All he got was enough to cover his medical bills. But he did not stop there. He went on to claim that in the process of transporting the injured, all his money fell from his pocket and he needed compensation. I could not say how that ended, but I am sure that, as far as I know, he did not hit the big one.

THIS IS KINGSTON HARBOR

During the good times, when the Oracabessa seaport was in full swing, drama was regular cargo and stowing away on a boat, to just about any country, was a way of life. These two coworkers planned long and hard for their great adventure. Everything was in place. The last two friends of theirs had made it to the U.S, and even wrote encouraging them to take the chance. So for them, there was no turning back. While loading bananas onto a boat, they carefully selected their hiding spot at a point where there was glass where light would shine through, when the boat docked at any port.

They boarded and after what seemed like an eternity in the dark timeless abyss, light finally appeared, foreign at last. That was approximately two hours after their departure from Oracabessa. The new arrivals then cautiously made their exit from the ship and entered the boardwalk. They had just succeeded in entering the harbor, when the first person they ran into was an old acquaintance they had not seen in years. "Heh my brotha, how are yah?" the first one said. The old acquaintance was puzzled and did not know how to respond. But before he could make anything of it, the other twanging accomplice declared, "I had missed ya for a whoile, but I did not know you were in the Stoites." "Which States?" the gentleman asked. "You damn fools, this is Kingston Harbor!" They simply left Jamaica and went to Kingston.

APPORKIATION

The meetings of our most esteemed political leader cousins, would always provide fodder for our hungry humor reservoir, and one of the most legendary was that of a luncheon that both attended at Kings House. It is always the common belief that Cousin B had the wit, while his cousin had the brain. They were both expected to address the luncheon, but Cousin Norm would go first. Norm, with his typical eloquence, began his speech by saying that it gave him great pleasure to 'officiate' in such capacity, so on and so forth. Cousin B was impressed with the speech, but especially, with the big word 'officiate'. He was wondering where his cousin got it from. In his frustrated state, he looked across and realized that Norm was having fish. That could explain it, he thought. He needed to match that speech. He was having pork for entrée. He rose and in the most confident and forceful of air, declared that like his cousin, it gave him great pleasure to 'apporkiate' in such capacity.

SAME JOHN CHEWY

This time both men were guests of the Chinese Embassy and the menu was all Chinese dishes. The order was being taken after the appetizer and when Norm was asked what dish he preferred, he replied 'Chop Suey,' Cousin B simply did not know how to pronounce the names of the dishes, let alone know what they really were, so he decided to play it safe. When he was asked what dish he was having, he replied; 'the same John Chewy, like my dear cousin.'

SKIP SIR B

I guess after all that exotic gorging, Sir B. saw the need to visit the doctor for his regular checkup. He was carefully examined and the medic felt he could lose a few pounds. He also prescribed some medication for a slight skin rash. As Sir B. was being handed the medication, the doctor instructed him to take the dosage on alternate days. The word alternate, was strange to Sir B, so he asked for a clarification. The patient doctor carefully explained that he should take the medication one day and skip the other and so on and so forth. Sir B was convinced

On his way home, he stopped at a haberdashery and purchased a length of rope. On his arrival home, Lady B. was curious and asked him about the rope. He apprised her of the doctor's instructions. She was happy for him and wished him well.

Sir B took the first dosage the same day. The next day, bright and early, he was up with the sun and he skipped from his back porch and around the entire yard like a boxer in training. Lady B. was delighted. The next day Sir B, did no skipping. But he was on queue the following day and the alternative days until his return visit to the doctor.

Had it not been for his very discernable features, especially his hair, the doctor could never have recognized the slim feature of the man who was approaching his office. Well, Sir B. thanked him profusely for his advice and the doctor was grateful but curious. Were those pills the new miracle drugs for obesity? And was Sir B. the inadvertent Guinea Pig? That poor doctor knew nothing about the rope and all the skipping.

I AM NOT STUPID

It was a landmark case in London and the lawyer representing the multinational pharmaceutical company was no other than the eminent Queens Council, Cousin Norm.

Needless to say the presiding judge had a superiority complex and had grossly underestimated the ingenuity of Sir Norm. At a certain juncture of the hearing the judge was as firm as a rock on a position he had taken and things were not boding well for Sir Norm's case. If he could not find some way to break the judge's hard stance, his case would be lost, and he found it when he gave a deliberately weird remark in response to a statement from the opposing bench.

The judge quickly admonished him for making a stupid remark, to which Sir Norm replied loudly; "I am not as stupid as Your Honor." and lowering his voice out of hearing of the judge continued, "thinks me to be."

The judge was livid and lost no time in doing a reprimand, which would precede a Contempt of Court charge. But the Clerk of Court was forced to interrupt the angry judge, and informed him that he had not quoted Sir Norm's remark correctly, as what he had said was that he was not as stupid as Your Honor thought him to be.

The courtroom almost fell into disarray as the judge scrambled to regain composure and Sir Norm seized the moment and eventually won the case.

HIDE AND SEEK BELLEVIEW STYLE

The two mental patients were friends and they played all kinds of games with each other. But their favorite was 'hide and seek'. One morning they were playing some other games and they decided to take a break. They had planned that after the break, they would play their favorite game. During the break, one of them felt tired and went for a doze under a tree. After the break, his friend searched frantically for him and eventually found him still asleep under the tree. He saw this as an opportunity to play a trick on him. Grinning with excitement, as was usual for them, he proceeded to use a cutlass that he was working with, and severed the head of his friend, hid it behind the said tree, and loudly declared that he would like to see how he would find it when he got up.

GEOGRAPHY 101

Where is Shae-Shae-Cum-Dung? I know it is somewhere near Gayle in St Mary. And where is Wappen Step? It was once Weeping Stairs. It is a steep shortcut at a very deep curve near Guys Hill in St Mary. You may have heard about the Sambo and Tiger (Sambre and Tiber) rivers. I have listened to them for years. These rivers crash together in Wood Park near Gayle in Saint Mary. When it rains profusely, the roars can be heard for miles.

Speaking of Wood Park, it is blessed with some conveniently placed neighbors; Cocks Piece, and Maiden Hall close by. Was there implied perversion on the namers' parts? No pun intended.

NOWHERE NEAR

The long time female resident in Saint Andrew simply did not like the new neighbor whom she thought did not fit into the mold of her upscale suburban neighborhood. He was not of the gentry so he could be a liability. She wasted no time to launch an assault on the unwitting newcomer. The new neighbor bred horses like most of the neighbors, but she would complain about everything. She even went as far as to breach the fence and allow his horses to stray. She lived alone and was not really well liked by those around her, so after all her attempts at mobilizing some actions against her new neighbor, had failed, she decided to go solo.

She filed a civil suit claiming that the neighbor's horse had kicked her and she even had a medical report to support it. During the trial it was clear that her version of events was full of holes and when she was interrogated, she was forced to admit that the fence on her side was not breached, so the horses could not leave their owners property. So how could she have gotten kicked? She would most likely have trespassed onto that property. The presiding judge in his summation reiterated the fact that for the complainant or anyone for that matter, to be kicked, he or she had to be near the animal. He continued that the complainant could never be near the horses if she was not on the neighbor's property and that would constitute trespassing. Realizing that she had dug herself into a larger hole, she had just started to contemplate a way out when the judge calmly asked her "My good lady, were you anywhere near that horse when it kicked you?" Her impulsive reply was "No your Honor, no!"

THE BIG CATCH

Ed and I were fishing in the White River near our home in Saint Mary. We were not having much luck at first, but it all changed when we came upon a fairly deep pool loaded with some very large perch. We threw our lines in and as fast as they were in, the worms were removed and no fish was hooked. It was getting very frustrating for me and I had to come up with a plan. The pool was fairly deep but the water was clear enough for the fishes to be visible when they came towards the hooks. The worm baits were pink and very visible in the deep water. As I watched, I noticed that the worms would disappear but there would be no jerk on the line, indicating a fish bite. The huge fishes somehow, craftily managed to get the hooks into their mouths and remove the worm undetected. That gave me an idea. I figured out that when the pink worm disappeared, that would be the time to pull my line as the hook would have been in the fish's mouth. I was right. The first time I tested the theory, I brought up my first big fish and in no time I had most of the huge perches on my string. My friend was having no such luck and selfishness made me not reveal my secret.

I was close to catching just about every large fish from that pool, when I heard my friend behind me give off a jubilant shout as he pulled in his first big haul. But as the fish landed, I observed that it was not struggling and jumping like a freshly caught fish was supposed to. I went over to inspect the catch and there were signs of dehydration on than lousy fish. That made me check the fishes on my string and lo and behold one of my large catches was missing. I confronted Ed, who laughingly told me that he had realized that he would become the laughing stock of the village, if I went home with all the big fishes and he with none. So to save himself the embarrassment, he had removed the fish from my string when I was not looking and hooked it onto his line and slid it into the water. He did not escape the ridicule for weeks to come.

CRICKET MATCH IN HEAVEN

This was one of the great one day cricket finals which are held annually in heaven. Satan appeared at the gates and Saint Peter spotted him right away, despite his disguise as Michael Jackson. The gloved one was already admitted to perform at lunch break. As the devil approached the eminent gatekeeper, Saint Peter declared "No, no, not again!" Satan clearly understood what that meant. Last year, after prolonged pleading, he was allowed in as Bob Marley, dreads and all, with the promise to behave himself with the motto 'One Love' but he did not. For no sooner had he entered the gates and saw the guards, he began to sing 'I shot the Sheriff.' and he was unceremoniously given the boot before God even realized what was taking place, and Saint Peter was spared his job. This time however, he was not prepared to risk it and he told Lucifer so in no uncertain terms.

But the word 'Lucifer,' conjured up old images and Saint Peter was having a dramatic flash back. Satan was supposed to be the reference, not Lucifer. Before Satan's name was changed, Peter and Lucifer were bosom buddies, even up to the denial of Jesus. So now Saint Peter was faced with the difficult decision once again and he pondered a way out. Just when he was about to render his decision to err on the side of caution and reject the entry, he overheard Satan humming one of their favorite pieces; 'Jah is My Keeper,' from Peter Tosh's Bush Doctor Album. That did it for Saint Peter; Satan knew how to evoke emotions. The song also gave St Peter the idea to admit Satan, disguised as Peter Tosh, with the promise not to burn any chalice inna the Heavenly palace.

As Satan made his entry into the field, he was just in time to hear the announcer say 'And now, in comes Solomon bowling to Sampson, and Sampson steps forward and he drives.' The ball was hit hard and high and as it came over to where Satan had reached, he began sprinting towards the direction of the ball holding his hand over his eyes to block out the sun. He was shouting something and as Saint Peter listened he clearly overheard Satan over the cheers declare "A tell you that that ('r' rated) man a go lick weh dat ('b'rated 'c') ball" "Same dyam ting a tell you man." declared Saint Peter, "That man never keep a promise."

CAMOUFLAGE

I see all these seemingly invincible military powers of the world wearing their perfectly designed camouflage and wonder if they ever had the slightest clue as to the origin of this great concept. I'll begin by taking you on a trip to Jamaica to visit some of the Maroon villages across the island. Except for some modern day amenities, not a lot have changed in these villages since slavery. Although slavery has been abolished and there is no need for resistance, I still believe the spirits of the long dead maroons like Nanny, and Cudjoe, still hover in these mountains, still guarding their hard earned freedom. The history of the island is decorated with the prowess of the Maroons much more than the uniforms of their arch rivals, the British Redcoats.

Emancipation did not come easily for Jamaica and I credit direct physical resistance from every corner for expediting the process. I also give credit to the intellectual and religious wings for their involvement. But as my intention here is not to bore anyone with bland history, I will get back to the task at hand

In school, I learnt that Nanny was a wizard who mesmerized everyone with her elusive power. We were taught that when the British Redcoat Soldiers launched an attack in the mountains where she resided, she would show herself to the soldiers who would fire at her and feel certain that they had shot her. What they did not know was that visions of her were like holograms. And she was merely a distraction for her fighters to set up strategic traps, the most effective of which was the camouflage trap.

As the soldiers pursued the Maroons, they would become tired and needed rest and shade. The Maroons did not have the means to outgun the Redcoats, so they had to devise means to get close to them to use their arrows or spears. One way they figured out to achieve this objective, was to simply become the small trees in the hills and the soldiers, not knowing this, would walk closely to what they thought were trees, only to be stabbed to death and their arms taken. The Maroons did not make the uniforms; they just blended into the environment. Eventually, the soldiers figured this out and the concept spread. But I was not done with Queen Nanny yet. What I was also taught, was that if and when she was cornered, she would simply catch the bullets with her mouth and spat them out in rapid succession. But as I grew up, the theory got juicier and if white rum was involved, even smutty. She did not really use her mouth, but all the bullets were discharged in rapid succession, to the detriment of the Redcoats

FIGHT THE GOOD FIGHT

It was a P.T.A meeting at my alma mater in Labyrinth Saint Mary and the group was celebrating a very successful fundraising venture that was held the week before. Everyone was happy and they were expressing it in their own way, one speech after the other. Some were eloquent while others were halting. Our most esteemed community grocer listened intently to the speeches, not so much for substance but for correctness. She had decided that a P.T.A meeting was no place for bad grammar

One very popular male senior's dad, who was himself respected and loved by just about everyone, ended his speech by saying and I quote "Brothers and sisters, we have fight a good fight and in the near future we hope to fight another one." That was followed by great applause from those in attendance. But while some of the members present thought little of the error, Mrs. Prim and Proper was overheard musing in no uncertain terms, so when her time came, she apparently seized the opportunity to set things right.

Our most esteemed grocer now rose to her feet and, in her typical form, gave an impressive overview of the event. In closing, she declared, she would like to quote a previous speaker: "We have fought a good fought and in the near future we hope to fought another one." (He just did not use his past tense right) The attending students were lucky that the clapping drowned their outburst, and it became the joke of the school for a very long time.

JUDGE DREAD

He was rushing to get to court in Spanish Town on this Friday morning, as he knew he would be facing the most feared judge in all of Jamaica. He thanked his lucky stars when the first car he flagged down, stopped to give him a ride. As he hastily boarded the car he said good morning and thanked the formally dressed gentleman for sparing him the misfortune of being late for court as that, (r rated) judge (and he apologized for the obscenity) didn't run any joke. He was so serious that he would fine himself if he were late for a minute and he would even take the money from his wallet and hand to the clerk right there in court for all to see. So one can imagine what he would have done to him if he were late.

For the duration of the short trip from Crescent, he recited incident after incident of the judge's reputed rulings, while his listener only smiled and mumbled a few words. He was finally dropped off in front of the court house and he rushed to get a seat to await his hearing. The criminal cases were finished and it was now time for the traffic cases. When his name was called, the traveler nervously stepped towards the bench. As he stood there, the arrival of the traffic judge was being announced. When the door opened, the regaled judge that walked to the bench, to the defendant's horror, was the said gentleman who gave him a ride earlier that morning. That was Judge Dread in the flesh.

The judge looked down and smiled at the nervous wreck, who could hardly pronounce his own name when he was asked. But as he braced for the worst, he got the surprise of his life. The calm, smiling judge dismissed his entire case with a warning to drive more carefully. But in his state of shock, the freed man almost crashed into a bench as he exited the courthouse. The judge was not offended by the rider's harsh rhetoric at all. He loved his reputation being sung abroad, profanely or not.

GUNS
BY LENWORTH HENRY

Guns do not kill, people do
I know you've heard that rationale too
Who in his right mind could contend?
That a gun is more weapon than a friend?

It's in whose hand the weapon falls
That makes it any threat at all
It's built to save humanity
And help enhance security

But I was young now growing old
The story needs again be told
A gun's a weapon made to kill
Has gotten more potent and it still

Leaves shattered lives and mangled frame
Outdoing its fore-bears, gaining fame
A thousand rounds within the minute
Blasting a trail and all those in it

Bang, bang, bang and rat-a-tat-tat
Ultimate power to an idiot.

WHAT CAR WOULD JESUS DRIVE?

That question came up a few years ago in the U, S, and I was surprised that people did not really know that simple answer, knowing this is a strong Christian nation. It is the Accord of course.

In the Upper Room in Jerusalem, Jesus and his twelve disciples were in one accord, according to the biblical account. Some news reporter could have gotten a little vague in his account. As a Jamaican, that comes as no surprise to me, as I remember the days when there were not so many cars on the island. Thirteen people were no match for an Accord, especially when it was plying the Spanish Town to Point Hill route. And the Honda Accord, to me, is amongst the greatest cars ever built. There are few cars that can match the durability of an Accord. And you need not mention their resale value. Service them right and they will take you, from here to eternity, from where we all came.